The Cost

By Cher

Graiden

Acknowledgments

To Cris Cole my very talented friend, without your patience in assisting me to finalise the story and your endless supply of profiteroles I may never have had this completed.

Also thank you to Becca for putting up with my constant requests for help with the computer, your tolerance is appreciated more than you could ever know.

Cher

"Have you heard yourself? You sound like someone in a cheap woman's magazine, 'true life stories of a mug.'

Those words have swum around and around in my head so many times and for so many years. I am not a foolish woman in fact I would say I was pretty intelligent. I have a master's degree and a highly skilled job. I am in charge at work, people look to me for guidance and instruction. I have brought up a family pretty much single handedly. This stuff only happens to foolish desperate women, or so I was convinced until I stood in the very shoes of the women I judged. I was that woman. How did I let it get to this and how the hell do I get back?

Introduction

"Hammett"

"Hammett"

"It's me, its Monica."

"Can you hear me Hammett?

"Can you see me?"

"Can you talk?"

"Try and keep calm and tell me what's happening, these people are here to help you, to help us both."
It was the early hours of the morning on the 1st November yet the rain fell that morning like a stormy winters day.

Blood mixed with the rainwater on the paving below his feet. He stood facing the railings he was holding onto like a caged animal. He shouted "Daye! Daye! Daye!" He stared forward at the railings. I was only able to see the left side of his face.

"Hammett! Hammett! It's me - Monica. Can you hear me, Hammett? Can you see me?"

He raised his left leg slightly and then lowered it. Then again, he repeated this simple process as if it were a complex challenge. He screamed out as he lifted his leg, his pain was unbearable.

"What's he saying, Monica?" The policewoman asked me as I walked slowly and cautiously toward him.

"He's shouting for his mother," I answered, I felt sick at the desperation in his words.

The policewoman put her hand on my shoulder reminding me that she was there. "Don't go too close, Monica. Keep the distance you have now. We need you to remain safe."

Two further police cars pulled up behind the police van. Their sirens were silenced by the hand gesture of the crew already present. The situation was volatile – no-one knew what had happened, and no-one could get close to him to find out. His level of aggression was intense.

"Please, Hammett, talk to me? These people are here to help you. Hammett, you're injured, and we need to help you." The ambulance turned the corner and reversed into the car park of the car park, twenty yards from where he stood.

"Ambulance on standby…" A message came over the police radio.

"It's time to move to a safe distance, Monica. The ambulance crew are here - we must let them do their job." The police officer held my arm to guide me away.

"Please, Hammett? Please?" I cried out. In that instance he very slowly turned his head towards me.

I could hear myself scream, but no noise seemed to leave my mouth. It felt like time had stopped as I wretched and vomited. The socket of his left eye was smashed so much it was difficult to see where his eye once was. A large pocket of skin had formed a bag of blood that hung from his face like something from a horror film. Blood sputtered from his mouth as he shouted "Daye! Daye! Daye!

Within what seemed like hours (but merely only seconds) three policeman grappled him to the floor. He screamed in pain as he was searched and hobbled towards the awaiting stretcher. The police officer held him upright at each side under Hammett's arms. They had to talk him through the process of taking one step and following it with another.

"How the hell is he still alive?" I overheard a police officer saying to her colleague. I stared in silence my body was in shock and my mind a blur.

He was strapped to the waiting stretcher as a large pad was placed gently onto his face, while the ambulancemen tried to work out how they could attach the pad without causing more damage.

I sat in the back of a police car following a very slow-moving ambulance with sirens blazing, as if it was undecided if to hurry or not. Twice on route the ambulance stopped while the ambulance driver had to assist the paramedic before they set off again ever so slowly. The police radio seemed to blast into the deafening silence of my head. We were heading to a distance hospital to a specialist head injury unit. But mid-journey it was decided he would not be able to survive the distance. So, we were re-routed to the nearest local hospital where a team of specialists were to be waiting.

Chapter 1

The telephone on my desk rang for what felt like the fiftieth time that day. It was late afternoon and for a few seconds I tried using my non-existent telepathic powers to will it to stop ringing, but it did not stop.

Leanne looked over from her computer, "Your phone is ringing."

"Yes, thank you, Leanne. I am not deaf - I was just busy with something."

"Well, it's still ringing," she said as she sat back in her chair, picking up her mobile phone to take yet another 'selfie.'

I rolled my eyes at her as I picked up the receiver.

"You took your time answering? I've been ringing for ten minutes."

"Hello, Belinda. It wasn't ten minutes and you know I can't talk at work. Is something wrong? Have you won the lottery?" I asked in a sarcastic tone.

"No, Monica, but I have done the next best thing," Belinda said with an excited tone in her voice.

There was a silence between us for a few seconds, which seemed like minutes. I knew it was my turn to ask what the surprise was, but I was in such a bad mood that day that I could not bring myself to speak. I was not interested in her surprises. In fact, I had enjoyed the notion that she had recently been on holiday. It was a break from her constant moaning and malicious gossip that seemed to be her fundamental purpose in life. Although we had been friends for several years, I felt as if time spent with her was more of a tolerance than a pleasure.

"Well, I'm not going to tell you what it is, but I will give you a little clue - 'extra leg room'."

I rolled my eyes again knowing full well she had booked us a holiday, one that I had no time for. These days I could hardly muster up the effort to get out of my bed in a morning. I often finished work and changed straight into my pajamas and liked it that way.

"I don't have enough holidays left at work to take, Belinda. I can't possibly come!" (I thought that was a great 'get out' clause).

"I knew you would say that, so it's all sorted. I've spoken to human resources and you've been given time off to visit your sick grandmother," Belinda answered, sounding very proud of herself in her achievements.

"That'll be the sick grandmother I haven't got, then?" I asked sarcastically.

I looked over and Leanne was staring at me through the gap between our computers and taking in every word of the conversation.

"I must go - I have to work. Speak to you tonight," I said abruptly and put down the receiver.

"Don't look at me like that, Leanne. Get on with what you should be doing and put your mobile phone away - you know it's against policy."

Leanne rolled her eyes and swivelled her chair, so she no longer had to have eye contact with me. She mumbled under her breath, "So is telling lies to get days off." Leanne had been my personal assistant for seven months. I had taken a likening to her at interview, impressed by her smart appearance and youthful energy - the same youthful energy that now made me feel 'prehistoric'. Her respect for me as her boss had waned, somewhat. I proceeded to ignore her comments, as I knew she was correct but could not stand to lose face in front of her once again.

Work on this particular day seemed like a lifetime and I was glad to leave at the end of the day.

Phil rang as I drove home, "Hello Hinny how are you?" Phil had been my friend for over a decade. We met at a works party where Phil had been on a date with Alistair from finance. He joined him at the party as his 'plus one' even though they had only been seeing each other for a few months. Phil had taken the invitation as a sign they were a serious couple and had dreams of a wedding and having two small dogs in a house in Chelsea. Alistair had other ideas, and left Phil standing in tears as he openly flirted with Annalisa Thornton-Wood, vice principal of the company.

Phil and I spent that evening in the women's toilets drinking wine and declaring all men bastards. Annalisa and Alistair later became engaged, even though Alistair admitted to Phil that he was with her for the money and the lifestyle. Phil had never really got over Alistair and he was always the brunt of our drunken conversations. Phil became my friend for life. We talked about anything and everything for hours on end. My parents were prejudiced against gay people and would not even have the issue of being gay discussed in our home, but they somehow over looked this when they met Phil and completely fell in love with him. Mum would ask how he was more than she would ask about me, she would come to life around him and ask his opinion on everything, as if his answers where the gospel. His comments of, "Janice, that dress is divine" and "Morris, you do look dapper in that suit" made them both positively gush with pride. He was invited to every family get together and even helped mum decorate her Christmas tree, which was the greatest acknowledgement of acceptance that she could bestow.

"I wanted to warn you first, but she made me promise to keep my mouth zipped- shut. She has booked you a week's holiday in Marmaris in Turkey. You hate it there, I know you do. She's up to something, I'm sure of it, and I know she's a friend, hinny but take care there."

"I'm devastated, Phil, but I'm going to have to go with her - I feel so obliged. It's very nice of her to do this, but it's such a difficult time to be away from work and she has no appreciation of how demanding my work is. Also, I don't appreciate it that she told lies to get me time off."

Belinda had not worked for several years. She had previously worked for years in a department store as head window-dresser. Her design style was old-fashioned, (much like her) and it showed in her work. Eventually the store closed its doors to make way for a high-fashion clothing shop. Belinda was blessed with neither good looks nor a figure to die for. She was egg-shaped with legs shaped like upside down champagne bottles and her severely short, dark hair matched her austere personality. She lacked self-awareness, but overflowed with self-esteem, despite her looks. She was a sharp and judgmental woman, who was not averse to judging others against her own standards. She had been married for thirty-five years and lived a financially comfortable life. Her husband Colin had inherited a large amount of money that had allowed them both to stop working in their forties, with no worries of how the bills would be paid. Along with the end of her workdays was her concept of the time pressures at work. Choosing to go on a spur-of-the-moment holiday was no problem for her.

Belinda's opinionated attitude lost her lots of friends and at times she seemed a lonely woman. Her children were both in the Forces and rarely, if ever, visited her. Her relationship with her husband had been platonic for several years and they acted more like brother and sister than husband and wife. Holidays had become her thing in life - she had travelled abroad eight times in this year already.

One week later, and despite my moral high ground, I persevered with the lies at work, and by Monday we were on a flight to Turkey. Three times during the flight Belinda felt the need to remind me that she has purchased extra legroom for us both. She had an intense need for constant gratification and thanks for her benevolence. I found myself feeling angry with her for her belittling attitude. I had been angry a lot lately - often for no apparent reason, my self-esteem seemed to be at an all-time low and not for any apparent reason. Although life had been no more difficult than it normally was; I had no particular reason to complain.

There was a couple sat adjacent to us on the flight who were about to be married. I watched them as the stewardess made of a fuss of them both, with congratulations and champagne. I felt jealous as they giggled together and made plans for an exciting future. The bitter side of me wanted to stand up and shout out that they had no idea what they were letting themselves in for. They should stop now while they were happy. But I didn't. I sat quietly. They smiled as they looked our way, drawn by the noise of Belinda snoring. I politely smiled back and rolled my eyes at her. The extra leg-room was more helpful for her large backside and back as she slid down the seat and slept. Her short stubby legs still did not reach the seat in front.

"Would she like this blanket?" a voice said disturbing me from my trail of bitter thoughts. It was the bride to be. She was holding a white fleece blanket with 'bride' written on the corner in silver sequins.

"No, it's fine, but thank you for the offer. Anyway, you should hang onto that – it's a wedding keepsake."

I now felt guilty for my bitter thoughts and slumped down into my own seat, filling the extra legroom. My marriage had ended as it started - in a loveless way. Lilly who was no longer small or needed me was the only good thing to come out of our blessed union. My ex-husband's name was Jake and he was the most childish man you could ever wish not to meet. Strangely enough, the fun aspect of him was the one thing that attracted me to him, but as he grew older in years his childish manner stayed the same and became the one thing I was unable to tolerate. I had never regretted my divorce, but always felt as if I had somehow had my shot at happiness and failed miserably.

The call came for us to prepare to land, so I gently nudged Belinda to wake up and fasten her seatbelt. She carried on snoring, so I pushed at her shoulder and she still didn't awaken. The stewardess touched Belinda's hand saying, "We are due to start the descent - if you could fasten your belt, please?"

Belinda woke with a start, "I must've nodded off - you should have woken me." I rolled my eyes at her for the tenth time that day and fastened my seat belt. I glimpsed the groom holding his fiancée's hand tightly as we started to descend. I could not help thinking how nice it was to have someone who cared enough to do the little things that counted like that. Then my ears popped, and we rumbled onto the tarmac.

"You are going love the hotel it is beautiful." I stuck a finger in my ear and jostled it about, trying to make out what she was saying as her words blurred into mumbling.

"Sorry?"

"I said, you're going to love where we're staying – it's bloody well beautiful! The brochure doesn't do it justice. I've read all the reviews and we are in for a treat."

We were not in for a treat. In fact, our evening went from one disaster to the next calamity. A strike at the airport left us at the back of a queue of over three hundred people - all jammed into an over-crowded waiting area with no air conditioning.

The sight of the sunset was a welcome sight as we waited at airport control just as we thought that the sizzling air might become slightly cooler. We had landed at five o'clock and it was now nearly eight and the staff where just arriving to start moving the irate queue of holiday makers and crying bored children through passport control. Belinda was unusually patient as she was normally the first to complain a pastime that she enjoyed very much. It was strange to see her so calm.

Belinda stood to her feet and began to rummage through her handbag. "I almost forgot - I bought us a healing crystal," she said, with a large grin on her face.

"What do you want it to heal?" I asked.

"Well, your miserable mood would be a start. You're never happy. All you do is work, work and work. You need to let loose and enjoy life sometimes."

I felt like bouncing the crystal off her head as she swayed side to side describing the beautiful colours of the flowers in Turkey, and how marvellous the people all were. She stood to her feet, rambling on for a few minutes, until she was brought down to earth by the security guard who rudely demanded she move along the line calling her an 'old lady'.

I stood and gathered my things, throwing the crystal into the bottom of my bag, to never again to give it a second thought. "You've got too much time and too much money on your hands buying that kind of shit. Don't you know that they sell this stuff to people like you just to make money?"

"What do you mean - 'people like me?'"

"Gullible idiots who are easily parted from their money on a whim or belief. People like you are a big market in the consumer industry."

Belinda rolled her eyes at me. "At least I believe in something and I am open to finding love." I was stopped in my tracks by the meaning that was hidden within her comments.

"Love? Since when are you looking for love? I'm sure your Colin might have something to say about that, after a lifetime of suffering a marriage with you. You'll need a crystal ball to find anyone else who's as patient as him and willing to put up with you - never mind a little crystal." Belinda merely smiled smugly and glided through passport control.

A Turkish man in his mid-sixties stood behind the barrier with a sign saying 'Miss Belinda' written by hand on a card.

"That's me!" she screeched as she totted towards him on her dumpy legs. She aimed to look sophisticated but failed, dragging her overfull cases across the floor as though they were dead carcasses. I sniggered to myself as she tried to hand the man the cases, but he looked at them, looked at her, then promptly walked off, leaving her to struggle as she waddled on behind him.

Our waiting car was no limousine. It was a battered old fiesta with more rust on the bodywork than paint. We struggled to fit into the car and Belinda's barrel-shaped body allowed her to only fit into the front seat with very little dignity.
Her dumpy legs were her saving grace. As the driver pushed her forward in her seat to jam her oversized case onto the back seat, she still had legroom, whereas I had little space to sit and no access at all to a seatbelt.

"I feel like Carrie from Sex in the City," Belinda said, squealing with excitement as we set off.

"Except you're Belinda in Turkey and I'd rather have chocolate and a cup of tea than sex these days?"

"Speak for yourself. I am in my prime of life. Men go for women like me who know what they want in life. They don't all go for these young dumb girls - some men like a little bit of sophistication."

I tried to sit forward in my seat to show my surprise at her sudden change in attitude to life but was stuck behind two cases. If we had crashed I would have either been decapitated or completely safe if the car rolled, as I could not move an inch.

"Why are you going on like a teenager in love? I thought Colin was getting on your nerves?" I asked.

Belinda ignored my comments and took out an envelope from her bag. "We are traveling to the Knomay Hotel please, driver?" she said as she wafted the paper in front of his face.

"The Crown," he answered.

Belinda looked stern-faced as she said "No, the Knomay." She began to read from her information leaflet. "It's a five-star hotel, only twenty minutes' drive from the airport and situated one hundred meters away from the beach." She talked to him as if she was selling him a holiday.

In his best Pidgeon English, he tried to explain to her that the Knomay had been overbooked and that he had been told to take all passengers to The Crown until the next day, when the matter could be resolved. Despite Belinda's best efforts to complain, we were taken to the Crown Hotel. It was walking distance from the Knomay and owned by the same company, but there the similarities ended.

The Crown Hotel was a three-star establishment and a far cry from our desired image fed by the glossy brochure pictures. The hotel was situated behind a row of shops and restaurants in a three-story building. The facade was worn and old. Plaster had fallen from large parts of the balcony walls and still lay on the path, just as it had landed a while since. Industrial-sized garbage bins marked every corner of the hotel with rubbish spilling into the street, much to the delight of the numerous stray cats that foraged there. Washing which had been put out to dry in the shimmering heat, hung over all the broken balconies, with makeshift clothes lines blocking out most of the three-foot square windows.

Our driver ran over an old child's bike that had been abandoned in the road, and promptly stopped to get out and throw it across the path, cursing and swearing as it was swung through the air. A woman's voice cursed back in Turkish from behind a curtain of washing, but she did not bodily appear. I hoped and prayed as he got back into the car that this was not where we were staying for even one night and breathed a sigh of relief as he drove on. My hopes were very quickly dashed as he pulled around the corner and parked next to an overfull industrial garbage bin that shadowed the car.

I stood with little hope in my heart that things could get any better, as I listened to Belinda demand that he takes us to another hotel, as she told him she knew her legal rights. He neither listened nor cared as he threw our bags onto the road, telling her to take the matter up with the Knomay Manager. He handed her a key on a large wooden key ring that had the number thirteen burned into it in odd sized numbers.

"Let's just go and see this room, Belinda. To be honest, if the sheets are clean I'll sleep there and sort this mess out tomorrow. It's too hot to be dragging cases around in this heat and there isn't a taxi in sight."

We dragged our cases up two flights of crumbling stone steps, with each step seemingly deeper than the last. A stone caught in the wheel of my case as I dragged it along - the stone landing on a surface of missing tiles and uneven flooring. A man lay drunk in the doorway of the first flat at the top of the stairs, and no amount of "excuse me," by Belinda was going to move him to let us pass. We hoisted our cases over the top of him to find ourselves at number thirteen.

"Surely not?" I heard Belinda say as we opened the door. Belinda pushed passed me in the small passageway. "This can't be right? We simply can't stay in here! This is awful! I would rather sleep on the streets."

The apartment was made up of a small passageway covered by a dirty orange- flowered curtain, lynched from a wire by two rustic hooks. The room had twin beds pushed together, made up with clean sheets. A single double kitchen cabinet with green doors housed an electric hob with two circular rings - one of which was smashed and broken. An old-fashioned kettle stood on the ring with a whistle to indicate when the water was boiled. Two large, brown, velour curtains covered a wall on the far side of the room, hiding what I hoped would be a balcony, to let us escape the claustrophobic feeling of the little room. Sadly, that was not to be, and Belinda pulled back the curtains to expose lots of dust and a small long window at the top of the room that was quite unreachable.

In the corner of the room was a doorway with an unpainted hardwood door, hanging from one hinge. The door hid a two-foot square room with a toilet and a tiny sink. A small shower tray that had been cut to fit, stood in the corner of the room with a shower curtain that when pulled, covered the toilet, too.
"At least the bed is clean," I said as I examined the bed looking for small mercies. I pulled back the sheet to expose a dirty stained mattress. "I think I am going to be sick." I ran to the bathroom, clambering over the bed as I ran.

"Let's just get out of here and find a drink. We can sleep on our towels – it's nearly 8pm now. We can leave early in the morning. The staff in the Knomay will be busy this time of the day, and I am sick of dragging them bloody cases around."

It was the best thing I had heard Belinda say all day. We put down our cases and lay towels on the bed as preparation for sleep and left to find a bar.

We had passed a small, friendly-looking bar on our way in the taxi. We decided to wander along and see if we could find it. Everything seemed so much further away on foot, and Belinda's idea of high heels for her 'Sex in the City' look was a bad idea. Her blistering swollen feet forced her to abandon her shoes and walk barefoot. After about fifteen minutes of walking, we found the bar and its warm lighting, and plants in pots placed here and there made it a welcome sight from the Bronx in which we were staying. Turkish music played in the bar as families sat around the wooden tables enjoying food that smelled beautiful as we passed by to go to a table.

"Table for two, beautiful ladies?" I heard a waiter ask behind me. I cringed at the very words; I looked like I had been on a long-haul flight, and Belinda looked like a bloated old goat. Belinda blushed as if she believed his words.

"Why, thank you, good sir?" she said as we were sat in a comfortable corner of the restaurant.

"Can I get you a menu, beautiful ladies?" The waiter asked.

"First, can we have two sloe gins - large ones - while we decide?" Belinda asked.

"Menus would be great, thank you," I said, feeling like she was a little bit brash.

The first drink hardly touched the sides as we read through the menu. Belinda had been on a Turkish-speaking course for beginners and saw herself as a bit of a native as she tried to pronounce some of the Turkish translations from the menu.

"It's written in English just below. Why don't you read that? You sound stupid - you can't speak Turkish."

Belinda was never fazed by my comments and as always, would only roll her eyes. We were so hungry following our flight - it had been such a tiresome day. Everything on the menu sounded nice and it was difficult to choose. We were onto our third drink by the time the food arrived, and Belinda was feeling confidently fluent in Turkish. I could see the waiters sniggering at her confident but incompetent efforts to chat. Belinda sat back and held her bloated stomach.

"Well, I have eaten at many wonderful places in my life, but that meal was beautiful. This place is a little gem, but can I ask - why does this restaurant not have a name?" she asked the waiter.

"When the man names his boat, he has a love in mind and only that will do, so until that day she shall remain nameless. That's what the chef says, anyway," answered the waiter.

Belinda was impressed, "Oh, that is so romantic, don't you think?" I did not honour her question enough to feel it deserved an answer, so I kept quiet and left her to her romantic thoughts.

The waiter carried on cleaning our plates from the table. I imagined he had said that same phrase any number of times to any number of silly middle-aged women. Belinda was by now talking with a drunken slur to her voice. She grabbed at the young waiter's arm as he held the plates. He seemed disturbed by her forwardness but was unable to leave her grasp without dropping the plates.

"Tell the chef I send my compliments, young man." She then let go of his arm and ushered him to run along. "Go on, then, do as I say," she said rudely.

The waiter gathered the rest of the plates as he said, "The chef is a married man." Belinda was furious at his response and she once again grabbed his arm but in a much less jovial manner than before.

"I didn't ask if he was married. I asked to send him my compliments. Now tell the chef there is a British food critic in the restaurant and she would like a word with him."

The waiter scuttled off to the kitchen looking as embarrassed as I felt.

"Why do you tell such lies? It's embarrassing! He's only a young boy."

"Old enough to think he could insult me? I know these people - I understand their language and ways - you just leave this to me."

I stood to go to the Ladies. "Please behave while I go to the loo. The money's in my purse if he brings the bill while I'm gone."

A few minutes later I returned to the table. I could hear her chatting to someone. "Ci senior, porpavou." I heard her say. I cringed at her stupidity in her attempts to look intellectual. She was chatting to the chef who had come to our table to receive her compliments in person.

I pulled out my chair and sat as they carried on chatting together. Thankfully, her attempts at a foreign language had ended, but she proceeded to tell a series of lies, introducing herself as a food critic and blogger. He was obviously impressed by her fictitious role and proceeded to invite her back for a complimentary taster meal on the evening of her choosing.

He was a small man of only five-foot-six, with dark curly hair. He looked around about forty-five years old, but it was difficult to be accurate, as his skin was darkened with the sun and he had many facial lines. His eyes were dark brown, and he had an intense look about him. His conversation with Belinda was abruptly halted (much to her disgust) as in broken English he asked, "Who might you be, beautiful lady?" as he took my hand and kissed it.

Belinda found this type of charm irresistible. unlike me. I found it repulsive and very uncomfortable. I pulled my hand away and started to gather up our things to leave.

"We're not leaving yet." Belinda abruptly took my purse from my hand. "We're just getting to know this talented chef? Sorry, I didn't catch your name?" She said, gushingly.

"Hammett," he replied as he gestured over to the bar staff to bring some complimentary drinks to our table.

"Why, thank you, kind sir. I do hope you're not trying to bribe me in anyway?" Belinda asked him as she giggled like a little girl.

"A real man knows deep beauty when he sees it, madam," he said as he took her hand and kissed it. Her faced flushed with pink as she enjoyed his attention.

I stood to my feet. "Let's go before I throw up. I can't listen to this shite anymore."

Belinda quickly apologized for my rude manners and made her own apologies as we left the restaurant. We bickered all the way back to the hotel about the evening. It felt like the holiday was doomed to be a disaster. Thankfully, the cocktails buffered the experience of having to sleep in that sty of a room, and as fast as my head hit the flat, hard pillows, I was sound asleep.

I woke the next morning overheating as Belinda had attempted to boil water in the kettle on the electric stove. The heat in the room was unbearable as she attempted to turn off the electric ring, feeling the kettle must now be boiled, as she could no longer see anything in the room for steam.

"It's going to have to be black tea as we've got no milk, and as I am such a good friend to you, I've given you the best cup, as these two are the only ones we've got." Belinda handed me a china mug stamped with 'I love Turkey' at a squew-whiff angle across the front. She had a cup with a picture of a naked woman whose clothes disappeared with the heat of the water. She had found the cup in the bathroom and promised me that she had scrubbed it well before she used it.

Belinda laughed. "You're so over the top, Monica. Did you know the Turkish drink tea just like this? They call it 'chai'. I enjoy it - I think I could get a taste for it."

"It's just black tea, Belinda. You could have that at home at any time - it isn't anything special," I replied.

We drank up and packed up the few things we had unpacked and ordered a taxi to the Knomay Hotel. I was so relieved to leave that room, I felt like I needed an hour's soak in the shower to take away the old damp smell from the bedding.

Our taxi pulled up at the drive of the Knomay. It was beautiful - the brochure pictures did not do it justice. Even before I had taken the cases from the taxi, Belinda had strutted into the reception and was already complaining to the receptionist who looked very unprepared for her onslaught. His offers of an apology with an explanation that there had been exceptional circumstances was not enough to settle her wrath. He carried on, trying to resolve her issues, which were more successful than anticipated as he offered us both a free upgrade and a free session of our choice in the hotel spa.

With our luggage taken to our room, we enjoyed the luxuries that awaited us there. We looked in awe at our stylish large balcony and lay in the sun, commenting on the stunning view. Complimentary champagne and strawberries were sent to our room, much to our delight. Suddenly, the experience of the room the night before became funny, and the recollection of its ghastly appearance and abysmal furnishings gave us cause for hysterics. I don't suppose it had anything to do with the champagne?

As the bubbles rose to the top of the glass, I could feel the negativity lift from my very being. A hot shower with complimentary herbal shower cream and a pine nut hair mask became the order of the evening. We ordered room service as we sat out on the balcony, wearing only dressing gowns and towels twisted in turbans on our heads and we fully submersed ourselves into holiday relaxation mode. Chill....

Chapter 2

"Remind me again - why exactly aren't I relaxing on the beach, stretched out on a sun lounger with a gin right now?"

Belinda stopped her fast-paced walking, only to turn and roll her eyes at me.

"How far away is this meeting point?" I interjected again with a much sterner tone which would demand an answer.

"It's here, right here. Now stop moaning," Belinda answered as she sat herself comfortably on a line of large rocks like she was taking a seat at the dentist.

I took the opportunity of rest to reapply sun cream for yet the third time that morning. The cream felt as if it was melting from my face and although it was only morning, the sun was already very hot.

I took out my phone and checked the weather forecast. "Thirty-two degrees! I'm going to need factor five thousand at this rate. I can't afford more lines on my face - I already look like Mother Teresa, as it is."

Belinda paid no attention to my ranting and stood waiting for the bus as if she would see its arrival long before anyone else in the queue would.

"How did you know the bus was coming just then?' I asked as we boarded.

"It was due at ten past and the Turkish are meticulous for time-keeping," she answered confidently.

I was bemused by her answer. "The Turkish are meticulous for time-keeping? Since when has that ever been a fact? And I assume you mean the full country as a race?"

Belinda rolled her eyes at me as she squeezed herself into a seat. "Stop being so picky. I was just generalizing - merely making an observation, that's all, nothing more, and you are not the politically correct police. No wonder your life is a mess - you need to learn to not over-dramatize every little thing in life."

I first met Belinda twelve or thirteen years previously. We worked together. Well, not together, but at the same place. She sat opposite me and always had a telephone receiver and a pen in one hand and a slice of cake in the other.
We never really chatted unless it was about work. I knew she was married and had kids, but that was where my knowledge about her ended, not my cup of tea, as my mother used to say. We were chalk and cheese I enjoyed fashion and going out, she liked heavy make-up and cake. She used to carry a large, knitted shopping bag, with her handbag carried inside it. It had never occurred to me that she might be lonely.

My world crashed around me. Not only around me – I crashed, too. I was suddenly faced with nowhere to go, no-one to love and nothing but failure and despair. "You know, Monica, you can talk to me?" Belinda peered over the stack of files in front of her. "I'm fine!" I lied.

"I might be a lot of things, but stupid isn't one of them. Come with me…" Belinda led me away from the room into a little side room used for meetings.

"Now – what's up? I can see you've been crying. You've got mascara on your sleeve. Spill the beans." She held my hand and then I let go of all the emotions and frustrations I had been bottling up. Belinda sat and listened. She said nothing but let me continue until I was burnt out. I had nothing left to say.

"Listen," she said, "I haven't got all the answers, but come and stay with me for a bit. I've got a spare room and Colin won't mind."

"Are you sure?"

"Not another word…"

I stayed with Belinda and her family for six months. She was always brash and always spoke her mind. She helped me by telling me things as they were. I suppose some would say that she was cold and heartless, which she was, but to me, the woman was worthy of respect. A friendship was formed and sometimes I regret it. Other times, I am open to it and sometimes glad of it, but today, on this holiday, I was starting to think better of it…

We both fell silent as we travelled along chaotic main roads and eventually across bumpy waste ground, heading towards our destination. Belinda said it was good for us to broaden our minds and that we were going to learn some culture. One thing I had learned in my 'messy' life, was that culture meant different things to different people. Belinda made me feel uneasy.

I am sure I could have been mistaken for not realizing that we had arrived at our intended destination when we left the bus and formed an orderly queue to look at a pile of ruins in the shape of an uneven square. Now, I am not opposed to looking at ruins and I enjoy history, but this looked more like the site of new-build houses before the owner had gone bankrupt. No conversation was needed. My face spoke a thousand words. Belinda on the other hand burst into 'art critic' mode commenting on the beauty of the stones and the history that steeped from their layout.

I giggled inside when the tour guide explained that we were to walk to the actual architectural site. The walk would take about ten minutes given the age of the group and the length of their legs. Belinda did not laugh and merely joined the line of eager tourists all of them (unlike me) in search for real culture. Drinks would be provided on route.

The ten minutes' walk was more of a twenty-minute stumble over a lot of rocky waste ground. The guide marched with a long thin stick which had a red flag at the top as if to put it on top of Everest. He pointed out a number of times that we were to remember that we were in the 'red team' should we get lost.

"As I said - the Turkish are very organized," Belinda said, as if in some a way she had just proven something. Then she headed off making her way to the front of the group to listen to the guide and soak in her culture on a more personal basis. I could hear nothing at the back of the line. Eventually we stopped, and everyone put down their bags and found suitable stones on which to get sore bottoms.

The area resembled historical ruins rather than the previous building site. The ruins stretched for over half a mile, where once stood a magnificent castle. I shuffled a little closer, so I could actually hear what was being said. The tour guide was an elderly gentleman with a short-cut grey beard and long, dishevelled white hair. He was well-tanned and looked English and spoke with a strong English accent. He wore a grey linen suit jacket that covered a white t-shirt. He looked relaxed in his work as if he had been confidently doing it all his life and still found pleasure in it.

"Welcome, everyone, to the ruins of Birach," he said as he stood to his feet as if commanding a military manoeuvre. His voice was mesmerizing, with a low gravely, rasping tone.

I found myself transported back in time, making mental images from his words. He spoke of the legend a prince called Alid and young girl called Emel. She was the daughter of a shepherd. Alid had fallen in love with her after he saw her while travelling through the mountains tending her goats, I think. Their love was forbidden, not only by the King because of her poor status, but also by Emel's father, who felt wronged that his daughter would marry so young to a man who was twenty years her senior. The shepherd felt that his daughter should marry only for love and in his considered opinion, she was not able to love the prince due to his age. The views of the shepherd were considered an insult to the prince and therefore, also to the King, and for this he was sentenced to a grisly death.

Standing at the gallows, the shepherd put a curse on the prince stating that he would never find happiness in life. Alid and Emel, contrary to their parents' wishes, married. After years of marriage they were still not blessed with any children.

Alid became frustrated with Emel and as she grew a little older, her youthful looks began to fade. Alid became a cruel and embittered man and plotted the demise of his wife.

He took her into the deepest forest to be left alone to die. Racked with guilt and remorse for his actions, he gathered a party of hunters and returned to the forest to find her. After months of hunting they found the body of Emel and her new born son in the deepest forest. Broken-hearted, Alid returned to his home and in a fit of rage he started a fire in his castle and lost his life as it burned to the ground. Legend has it that the gods took the baby boy as a sacrifice for Emel's stolen youth.

I felt saddened and still lost in the legend as we were ushered back into line for the second half of the trip. This was to be a wander around the local market.

I boarded the bus feeling downhearted. The journey to the market was a short but quiet one. Belinda had purchased a small-engraved glass block from the site of the ruins. It depicted a picture of what the castle had once looked like.

"Why have you bought that?" I asked.

"I like it and it's a reminder of a love story," she answered.

"It's 'tatt' and a reminder of a sad story of a typical man taking what he wants and ruining a young girl's life. Another thing to dust" I replied.

We got off the charabanc and decided to avoid the crowds and stop for a coffee. A small basement café with table and chairs situated on its steps looked exactly what we were hoping for. The menu was printed in Turkish with English translations below each entry. Belinda attempted to ask for two café lattes in Turkish, but eventually gave up and pointed at the menu, much to the barman's relief.

"I don't know why you're doing that - you can't speak a word of the language and quite frankly, it's embarrassing," I said honestly.

"That is your opinion and it means nothing. I happen to know that people abroad very much appreciate the effort of outsiders trying to speak their native tongue."

Belinda quickly changed the subject, asking my opinion of the legend of the ruins.

"I don't know how much of the story is true, but I really found it sad. It was a story of exploitation and selfishness," I told her.

Belinda completely disagreed and found it to be a story of forbidden love. We discussed how we just see things so differently, finding myself slightly envious of Belinda's sudden rose-tinted view of life. I sat watching people busily go about their day at the market and love-struck couples who were obviously enjoying their time together. It made me contemplate why I could see no good in relationships?

An elderly couple walked by the café holding hands - obviously both retired but looking very fit and active. They chatted and laughed as they walked by and chatted with a lady on a fruit stall talking in Turkish to her.

"How lovely to grow old with someone like that? Don't you think so?" I asked Belinda, who was by now looking down at her phone smiling. "Are you even listening to me?" I asked her.

Belinda looked up from her phone to tell me that she was listening and yes, she thought it was nice that the couple had grown old together and still enjoyed life, but that it was obviously based on the right chemistry. I was taken aback by her blunt answer.

"Chemistry is what you have when you first meet someone. It's not what gets you through life together," I stated as if my opinion was factual.

Belinda sniggered to herself then said, "If the chemistry is there from the first, it's always there. What you're referring to, is lust - and therein lies the difference and the difference between us."

Our coffees arrived with two small plates of what I referred to as 'cakes' but I was quickly corrected by Belinda, as baklava - a local delicacy of which she knew all of nothing, but still more than me.

"What's this sudden interest and knowledge in all things Turkish, and your vast knowledge of true love?" I asked her.

She took a long slurp of her coffee, taking her time to answer my question.

"I just like it here, that's all. I feel like I have a connection with the place and with the people. I feel at home here," she answered.

"Why do I get the feeling there's something you're not telling me? "I asked.

Belinda sat forward in her chair and in a confident manner said, "It's late in life, and unexpected I know, but I have met the love of my life. There is an amazing chemistry between us. And before you ask – no, I'm not talking about Colin. I'm talking about Temarh."

"Who the hell is Temarh? And what about Colin – he's your husband!"

Belinda took another slug of her drink and sat back in her chair while she contemplated her response.

"Colin is a nice man and has been a good husband, but we are like brother and sister and have been for some years now. Splitting up was always a matter of finding the right time," she answered as if she was talking slowly to a child.

"Does Colin know about all this?" I asked.

Belinda took her time in replying and drank her coffee and looked around as if she somehow could take herself away from the conversation. She looked awkward, with that 'hunted rabbit' look in her eyes.

Her arrogance and lack of an answer angered me. "Belinda I am asking you a question. This is a big deal - have you even thought this through?"

"I have thought of little else since Temarh and I met. I know things won't be easy, but you only live once there's no second chance. And Temarh makes me feel so alive, he is such a passionate person. You need to meet him, then and you'll understand."

"I understand you're in some sort of a mid-life crisis and making a damned fool of yourself," I answered in anger at her flippant stupidity.

Not a word was spoken between us for the rest of the afternoon. We went our separate ways around the market, but I had no interest in purchasing souvenirs, cheap tack or tawdry baubles. I felt trapped in Turkey, as if in some way I had been taken there under false pretences. She had always been so stubborn and head-strong in life, but she was far from being a reckless woman. It was so difficult to believe that she could be so foolish. In a desperate need to tell someone, I rang Phil and told him what had happened. The phone call did not have the desired effect of calming me down. Phil said a number of "Good God's" and "Seriously?" as I told him her plans.

He told me how he had read of similar stories in magazines, of how women were duped and ended up losing everything, saying they often looked like a laughing-stock in the pictures. When a sixty-year-old woman is stood next to a twenty-year-old man declaring true love, they look absurd.

"You're not making me feel any better, Phil. I can't sit back and let her throw her whole life away."

"Sorry Hinny but it's in black and white in the magazines. How old is he?" he asked.

"I don't know - I didn't ask, but I'm sure that he's isn't a twenty-year-old man barely out of secondary school. She might be besotted, but she's not that stupid."
Phil simply said "hmmm" which spoke volumes.

When I arrived back at the bus she was sat in the window seat with carrier bags on the seat next to her. She lifted them up and placed them on her knee, as if to invite me to sit next to her. We sat silent for a few minutes until I asked, "How old is he?"

"What does that matter?" she answered avoiding the question.

"Well, if it doesn't matter you won't mind telling me, will you?" Belinda glared at me.
"He's nearly twenty-four, if you must know."

"That will mean he's twenty-three, then. I'm sure you're going to say he's very mature for his age, as well."

Belinda was not fazed. "I'm not going to explain myself at all. I'm in my fifties and I do not and never will need permission from you about who I do, or do not love."

"You're old enough to be his mother," I pointed out.

"And yet he fell in love with me. Well, doesn't that just go against the norm?" Belinda said sarcastically.

"He is younger than your kids! How the hell are you going to explain that to them."

"I'm not. Because just like me, they are grown adults and we don't have to explain our actions of choices to one other."

There was no further conversation on the journey back to the hotel. Tension between us in the hotel was taut and almost tangible. I flicked through internet pages mindlessly.

Belinda left the hotel room that night and was gone for hours. I showered and attempted to unwind but was overcome by a sudden wave of self-consciousness as I walked into the restaurant. It was packed full of couples in love and happy families.

Making no effort to fight my pathetic self, I retreated to my room and ordered room services. In a state of pure self-loathing I managed to consume a large bowl of chips and cheese, a multi-layered toasted sandwich and three sugar doughnuts.

Lying on the bed, exhausted after my trough for one, I decided to ring Belinda. Her phone went straight through to voicemail. I lay there for a while, flicking through the channels on the television. I found nothing worth watching and even less in English, except for an ancient episode of Take the High Road dubbed into Turkish. I felt as miserable as Mrs. Mack looked.

I tried again to call her, this time leaving a voicemail asking her to get in touch as I was now starting to feel concerned. I must have fallen asleep, when I was abruptly awoken by Belinda slamming the bathroom door. She went onto the balcony for a cigarette in her dressing gown with a towel turbaned onto her head. I could not bring myself to question where she had been. I turned over and fell back to sleep.

I woke in the morning, late. Belinda was sitting on the balcony smoking a cigarette, but this time she was dressed. She had ordered breakfast from room service for us both - fruit and tea were already on the small table. I opened the balcony door fully and sat in the white plastic chair next to her. We both voiced the word 'sorry' at the same time after which we both laughed out loud.

"Me first, I am sorry but I brought you here under false pretences and I should've come clean from the start. The thing is, if I had, you wouldn't've agreed to come with me, and it's really important to me that you meet him. We've been friends for many years and your opinion does matter to me."

"I know, and I can't say that I don't think all of this is foolish because I do, but I will meet him. You're right that my life is a mess, and I am an emotional wreck, so I have no right to judge you, really."

With hatchets buried, we decided to head off to the beach. We hired sun loungers that were closest to the sea, so we could enjoy an uninterrupted view of the beautiful island and the mountains beyond the horizon. Fuelled by cocktails, the day flew by quickly, as we dipped in and out of the sea and sunbathed at our leisure. Belinda talked about Temarh a little, explaining how she had met him as she lay around the pool while on holiday with Colin. It was a golfing holiday - a yearly event arranged by the Western Star Golf Club to which Colin was a lifelong member. Belinda never really mixed with the other golfing wives and referred to them as 'golfing black widows.'

Belinda's eyes sparkled as she spoke of Temarh and how she loved to listen to his views on life. He had made her feel special by paying attention to her when no-one else did. He took a keen interest in her life at home and talked about his wish to study in England and better himself. She described his handsome physique and youthful good looks. He paid attention to her and only her and was fazed by younger, fitter women around her.

With every word she spoke, I trusted him less and less. He had seen a vulnerable needy woman and said all the right things. I kept my opinions to myself as we sipped on cocktails and admired the view, but silently dreaded what it would do to her if I was right in my doubts. I looked at her smiling at the very thought of him. It made my heart sink with pity for her.

"I have arranged for us all to eat in a fabulous restaurant tonight. I can't wait to take you - I just know you will be blown away by the food," Belinda said excitedly. "It is a fish restaurant and the fish are literally fresh from the beach. I always choose the tomato salsa it's beautiful! I've asked for the recipe every time I have visited, but they'd never let me have it. The Turkish are very secretive about their recipes, you know?" The more Belinda tried to act intelligent and worldly the more ridiculous she sounded.

"I'm not overly keen on fish, Belinda. It can play havoc with my digestion if it's not cooked right."

"Trust me and don't worry it's cooked to perfection and so fresh it is practically swimming. The place is call Venhal. Their tables are pre-booked for most of the season and it's not cheap."

"How did you find the place?" I asked.

"Temarh loves it. It's is one of his favourite places to eat, and he's friends with the chef there. We're treated like royalty whenever we go there. He knows most people he is very popular."

I thought of asking if he ever paid for the meals, but it would just cause another argument and the day had been so relaxing, I didn't have either the energy or inclination for it.

We arrived to eat at eight that evening, and Belinda was not wrong about how lovely Venhal was. The seats were situated in the sand on the beach. Some of the tables were actually set in the slow rising tide of the sea, where diners could sit with feet in the shallow, lapping waves, waggling their feet.

The smell from the restaurant was exotic and aromatic. The choice of the menu left me very much undecided but knowing that whatever I chose I would want something else. Belinda spoke to the waiter in her broken attempts at Turkish and told him we had a table for three booked, stating that she would like her usual table that she preferred when she was here with her partner Temarh. The waiter looked at Belinda as if she had spoken an alien language as he escorted us to our table. Belinda was most perturbed that we were not sat at her 'usual' table but justified it by saying this was a new waiter she had never met, who was obviously a novice.

"It doesn't matter, this is a nice place to sit. The breeze from the sea is lovely and cooling," I said.

Belinda perused the menu telling me all about the meals she had had in the past and how nice they all were. The waiter attended our table and asked if we would like to order. Belinda very quickly ushered him away, telling him that she was expecting her husband to join us and that he had been delayed. She swiftly gave him an order for drinks and requested ice and lemon water for the table.

"You were a little abrupt with him there, Belinda! and what is with this husband business? Let's be honest here, this might be true love, but you are still married to Colin. Don't you think you're jumping the gun a little?" I asked.

"It was a just figure of speech, and anyway, that's how you have to speak to people here. It's the culture - you just don't understand it. He probably shouldn't be talking to me on my own without Temarh - it's seen as an insult and a bit forward by some."

I was too shocked to say much to that. I sat and thought. In a matter of two days, she had gone from being an independent woman with a husband and grown up children, to a pathetic woman, happy to hide in the shadows of a man she hardly knew.

"You're starting to scare me now, Belinda. Let's just verify things here. You are not married to this man and you are not a Muslim. You have never followed that religion or culture, so why the hell are you pretending to know things about a subject that you are so clearly ignorant of? While we are on the subject, when the hell were you the sort of woman who thinks she shouldn't be spoken to without the permission of a man?" I was furious at her inane response. For a few moments we sat in complete silence sipping our drinks.

"What time is he coming?" I asked.

"He said he would be here for around eight, but sometimes he's a little late because he is head barman at the hotel, but he more or less runs the place. He can never leave on time, they struggle to manage when he's not there."

I tried in vain not to roll my eyes, but I could not hold my facial opinion back. Every time she referred to him, he was the best of the best - she was completely blinded by love and could see nothing but good in him.

After an uncomfortable forty-five minutes and three requests from the waiter to give him an order, Belinda asked me to choose while she excused herself, taking her mobile phone with her. I could see her frantically attempting to contact him while she nervously puffed away on two cigarettes. After ten minutes she returned to the table looking nervous and unsettled, pushing her plate away as if she were unable to tolerate food. I could not bring myself to ask the obvious question and did not need to, as she started to make a steady stream of excuses as to the reasons he was unable to attend or answer his phone.

'They take the piss out of him at that hotel. He does the work of three men and he can never get away on time. He's too polite to say anything to stop them. He will've fallen asleep - he is exhausted working all the hours god sends trying to better his life. If he has gone to see his family, he won't use his phone, his father doesn't like them, and he would never disrespect his father." She continued, not believing a word she was saying. "I bet he has got the day wrong on the calendar - he has a terrible memory for dates. He is likely to be stood at the airport now waiting to pick me up. He'll be on the phone any minute now trying to find me." Belinda sniggered at the thought. My days of sniggering had passed.

Chapter 3

Dinner was a disaster, the food remained left uneaten. Temarh was nowhere to be seen. I sat with Belinda to the very end of the night while she drank her body weight in gin and made excuses for his absence. The waiters cleared tables around us and stood uncomfortably as they willed us to move and allow them to close. Even on the short walk back to our hotel, she thought she spotted him in the distance running towards her with apologies at the ready, but it was not to be. Unable to take any more disappointment she fell asleep on the bed in a drunken coma. I felt overwhelming pity for her as she lay face down into the mascara-stained pillow. Even in her sleep tears rolled from her eyes. The harsh reality was that he had stopped her from seeing a reflection in the mirror of a bored, overweight middle-aged woman. His attention gave her confidence and a new direction in life. But today, that direction was a long road to tearful sleep.

Belinda woke the next morning feeling as bad as she looked. She showered to try and freshen herself up while I made us a coffee. Her mobile phone had run out of battery power and she went into panic mode, she searched around to find a charger as she held the phone in her hand willing it to gain power quickly, so she could receive a message from Temarh. No messages were waiting to appear and reluctantly she stopped looking at the screen and went to the balcony for coffee and cigarettes. Belinda checked through Facebook for any clue to where he might be. She messaged friends of friends in the hope they may have some idea as to his whereabouts and with no response and dwindling hope she lit another cigarette.

"If you don't go easy on them cigarettes you will have died of cancer before you see him again," I said as I poured us both more coffee.

"I am worried, Monica. I have a feeling in my gut that something is very wrong. He would never let me down like that and not be in touch. He's just not that type of person," Belinda said as she took a large drag from her cigarette and then stubbed it out, playing with the ash in the ashtray.

"He must have family and friends here? Surely, they would've been in touch if something was wrong, I'm sure he is fine."

Belinda drew on another cigarette as she said "They wouldn't know how to contact me, he was keeping our relationship secret, not because he didn't want people to know, but because he wanted to tell his Mum at the right time and not have her hear it from anyone else. He said that his Mum would be upset if he married an English woman, as she would know that she would lose him. She has been ill lately and he did not want to exacerbate that."

I wanted to get hold of her and shake her into seeing sense, but she looked so despondent as she made excuse after excuse, sitting in a cloud of smoke. I found myself thinking of ways to help her find him. "We could go to the bar where he works? Surely they would know if he has been into work or not, or where we could find him?"

Belinda's eyes lit up. "Brilliant idea! I'll get dressed and order a taxi."

The journey was not far and Belinda had handed the fare over to the driver and leapt from the car the minute it had stopped. I followed her to the gates of the Halm Golf Club resort. The sign at the side of the gate boasted of acres of five-star golf provision with hotel and leisure facilities. The gates were over ten feet high with black imposing lion heads at the centre, a guard stood at the side of the gate and took our names, ringing ahead to state our entry. As we entered, a golf buggy drove towards us, ready to take us to the golf bar and pool.

"Beautiful day today, ladies," the driver said as he stepped out to open the door for us.

"Have you had the pleasure of staying here before, ladies, or is this your first time?" the driver asked as he drove along the winding path to the hotel.

Belinda started talking in what she thought was her posh voice pronouncing her 'h's' extensively.

"Once or twice - I really do not hactually recall hexactly. I have stayed in so many places like this you see, my husband is a keen sportsman and golfer."

"Very nice, madam - you sound very proud of him."

Belinda went quiet after his comment and I think she was embarrassed and felt that being quiet was best policy.

The hotel was a grand building with marble steps that led to its large entrance doors. The black and white tiled floor was framed by white columns covered in bright pink fresh flowers. Chandeliers hung from the ceiling and glistened in the sunlight. I suddenly felt much underdressed for the occasion, as we made our way through the hotel to the pool area. There would be no race to put towels on the sunbeds at this hotel, as each sunbed was a double bed with white wooden frames and surrounded by linen curtains to keep out the relentless heat. Each stood in its own little private area of garden within sight of the pool.

"This place is stunning Belinda," I commented.

She seemed unfazed by its beauty and replied, "Well, there's a lot of money in golf." She headed of towards the bar where two waiters were setting up for the day, cleaning glasses and slicing lemons.

"Can I get you something, madam? It is complete waiter service and can be brought to your lounger, if you would rather?"

"I'm not here as a guest – well, not today. I am looking for Temarh - he works here," Belinda answered.

Both men looked confused as they explained they worked in a team of three for the full summer and did not know Temarh or anyone of that name. They asked if he could have been one of the temporary cleaning boys, as they explained they often took on young staff for temporary cleaning work. Belinda was very upset that they should even suggest this and went on to explain that Temarh was head barman and practically ran the hotel, so they must surely know him?

"Do you have a picture, madam? Maybe one of the other staff in reception might know him?" the barman asked.

Belinda looked embarrassed as she took out her phone to find a slightly blurred picture of herself and Temarh, in which a large portion of his face was hidden, with large dark glasses and a blue sports cap pulled down over his forehead. The barmen looked at each other, and then politely said they were sure that he was not an employee of the hotel and apologized that they were not able to help us.

We left the hotel walking down the long winding path that we had been driven up earlier. Belinda was angry as she felt that the barmen knew something and that they were keeping something from her.

We stopped at a coffee shop a few hundred yards from the hotel gates, while Belinda examined the blisters to her feet. We sat at a table just outside the coffee shop under an umbrella to try and cool off from the glaring morning sun.

"Why would they keep anything from you? They may genuinely not know him?" I suggested.

"Trust me they know him. And you may think it is far-fetched, but he mentioned to me that he had got involved in some debt, trying to pay for his mother's medical bills and he had struggled to pay. He told me that debt collectors over here are nothing short of the mafia."

"Oh, Belinda, you're making a fool of yourself! Surely you don't for one minute believe he has been taken by the Turkish mafia?" I said as I buried my head into my hands with despair.

Belinda defended her stupid ideas, "You don't understand how things work here – it's a completely different culture."

"Has he asked you for money?"

"No, he hasn't and he never would. He is too proud and he is not after my money, so get that idea out of your head." Belinda's answer was one of anger.

"Okay then, I'll rephrase that - have you sent him any money?"

Belinda lit up a cigarette as she said, "It's my money and I will do whatever I wish with it." She had sent him money and not for the first time. She had wired him eight hundred pounds the day before we arrived on holiday. She made no mental connection to the fact that she had sent him money and he was missing. She went on to defend his honour describing him as 'not being a money-driven person' but as a man who lives life to its full and is not guided or driven by finances.

"Why does he need your money if he is not held back by finances?" I asked.

"He didn't ask for money - I offered it. And I know for a fact, that he has used up all of his saving for his studies and to pay medical bills for his mother. His education is our future, so in essence I am investing in myself and helping his family at the same time. In fact, I love that he is honourable and selflessly helps his mother like that. He doesn't like using my money - he is a very proud man and if you must know, he begged me not to send it."

We sat for a while ordering extra cool drinks while Belinda rang Temarh's number and sent numerous texts.

"Why don't we go to his home address?" I asked.

Belinda did not answer my question but carried on checking her phone in the hope of some reply from him.

"Belinda, why don't we try his home address?" I repeated.
Belinda seemed agitated by my question. "He is a nomadic type of man - he just stays with friends. He wouldn't waste money on rent when he knows it takes away from his finances he needs for his studies. Anyhow, he always wanted to stay with me when we were together." Despite her flimsy defence, even Belinda was starting to know things were not looking good.

We agreed to go back to the hotel and see if there were any messages at reception and then make a plan from there. I spent the afternoon lolling around the pool and enjoying the sunshine, while Belinda sat on the balcony smoking cigarettes as she foraged through Facebook and Instagram in the hope of finding a clue to his whereabouts. By late afternoon, Belinda decided things had taken a serious turn and she had convinced herself that Temarh was hurt. She had decided that if he were indeed a conman, as I suspected, then there would be trace of him on social media.   In the absence of such evidence, she had come to the conclusion that he was hurt and therefore physically unable to contact her.

Now with an increased sense of urgency, boosted by an unwavering belief of tragedy, we headed off to find the local police station, to file a missing person's report. Nothing that I could or would have said to her would make any difference to her view that Temarh had been taken from her and kept against his will. We took a twenty-minute taxi ride to just outside the local bazaar, where the driver pointed us in the direction of the local police station. In broken English he tried to explain that the police station was at least fifteen minutes' walk up the bank and on cobbled paths, pointing at Belinda's kitten heels as he spoke. The fifteen-minute walk destined to be more of a forty-five-minute hike through cobbled streets, where little stone houses were built up on what felt like a ninety-degree angle. The initial comments of how pretty and quaint the houses looked with their brightly coloured flower boxes and doors quickly stopped as neither of us could breathe.

"I am so unfit, "I declared as I stopped to lean against a small wall so I could rest.

Assuring me that we did not have far to go, Belinda encouraged me to push on.
"I think we may have taken a wrong turn. It can't be this far, surely?" I stated as I stopped again attempting to adjust my shoe, no longer able to ignore the call of a throbbing blister.

Belinda ignored me and tottered on in front in her kitten heels. I noticed how extremely large her calves were as she walked in front of me. Her heels fell repeatedly between the cobbles causing her to wobble as she walked.

"The taxi driver said we were to turn right at that first street, and I am sure we turned left," I supported my case of being lost with my suspicions.

Belinda was obviously aggravated by my constant negativity. "My husband is missing and all you can do is moan about your blisters. Can you try and be a little less selfish, please?"

I did not have the breath to argue that he was not, in fact, her husband and probably never would be, as he had so obviously taken her money and ran, but I kept my mouth shut and walked on.

"Is that it down there?" I asked as we passed an alleyway.

"No," she replied bluntly as if I was obviously wrong. A stone stairway led down the alley to a blue door lit up by a faded blue light.

"I think it is the police station," I said as I stopped in my tracks, as if to demand attention with my physical protest.

Belinda ignored me and walked ahead stopping only to ask a lady unpacking her car taking groceries into her house. "Pardon, Madame, polis destination?" Belinda asked as I contemplated throwing myself down the nearest well in embarrassment of her attempts at Turkish.

A man came from the house to take the bags of groceries from his wife's full hands, looking suspiciously at Belinda as if she were insane. He closed the boot of the car and ushered his wife into the house. A young woman stood further down the road in a doorway smoking a cigarette. She was very young and slim, wearing jeans and a black vest, showing tattoos covering both her upper arms. She had dark hair pulled into a hair clip and piercing dark eyes.

"If it's the police station you are looking for, it's back down there to your left. It has a blue door. It is half way down the stone steps," she said as she took another drag from her cigarette and blew smoke rings into the air. She stubbed her cigarette out onto a small plate on the top of the wall. "I should warn you though, don't expect too much - they aren't like English police - you will be lucky if they are awake." Belinda attempted to thank her for her advice but before she had chance she had picked up the ash-ridden plate and entered the house saying "chow" as she closed the door.

We headed off down the stone steps and Belinda took the lead, knocking firmly on the blue door. A curtain twitched in the window to the left of the blue door, but no-one answered. Belinda knocked again as firmly as she had the first time. Still with no answer, she lifted the post box shouting "Hello!" through the opening. Belinda stumbled back on her little heels as the door suddenly opened as she attempted to view through the post box. Belinda gathered her composure. She straightened her clothes and tried to converse with the policeman who answered the door. He looked at her with a look of confusion as she attempted her broken Turkish, rudely leaving Belinda mid-sentence, he turned his back on her and walked back into the building. She tottered in after him and was bluntly stopped in her tracks as he lowered a panel from the wall, forcing her to stand the other side of the panel, as if to enforce his authority and distance.

Belinda carried on with her conversation, to which he said, "Sit!" as he pointed to two plastic chairs in the entrance. Like a pair of naughty schoolgirls, we immediately sat where we told to and he walked off into another room, across the corridor.

We sat quietly awaiting his return, we waited and waited until forty minutes had passed. We looked at our watches and spoke loudly as to attract attention, in case he had forgotten we were there, but it was to no avail. We sat for a further twenty minutes, not daring to knock on the door in case they were busy. Eventually the door opened and a policeman came to the counter. He looked scruffy, as if he had just been woken from a nap. His shirt collar was folded awkwardly to one side, and he had stains down the front of his jumper. He yawned loudly as he walked to the counter, he did not speak, but merely raised his head, as if giving us permission to speak.

Belinda stood to her feet and headed to the counter to commence her onslaught of important information, he stroked his thick dark moustache as she spoke, not saying a word in response. Belinda went on to tell a lengthy story of her missing true love and when she had finished, he continued to stare at her and not speak. We all stood silent for what seemed like ages until he stood up straight and walked to the door across the corridor and shouted, "English" to the policeman sat in the office.
A much smaller, balding policeman took his feet down from the desk on which they were resting and scuttled towards the counter.
"I can help you?" he asked.

Belinda looked furious as she once again attempted to give her account of events, as the policeman stood appearing to listen. After stating the full level of her events and the severity of her concerns, the policeman pushed a piece of blank paper across the desk with a pen and requested Belinda write down a statement. I sat back in the chair and contemplated how much time we were wasting. When she completed her statement, Belinda shouted for the attention of the policeman. With the door ajar, I could see the two policeman playing card games, as they sat with their feet resting on the desk, they ignored our requests for attention and carried on with their card game.

"How rude!" Belinda became angry at their lack of attention to her concerns.

The smaller policeman came to attend to our requests, slowly walking towards the counter as if he was in no hurry. "Thank you," he said as he took the paper and pen from Belinda's hand and placed it under the counter. The other policeman shouted something in Turkish from the other room, prompting the balding policeman to ask Temarh's age.

As she answered, a loud boom of laughter came from the other room. The smaller policeman smiled as he condescendingly assured Belinda that he was sure Temarh was safe and well and would turn up of his own accord very soon. The taller policeman shouted a further question in Turkish to his counterpart as we stood to leave, "when's your flight home?" he translated into English.

"Monday at eight thirty in the morning," Belinda replied. A voice from the other office could be heard with only the word 'Tuesday" translatable followed by raucous laughing.

Tears flowed from Belinda's eyes as we left the station, not only because of the humiliation that I had observed, but for the concern of Temarh's welfare, knowing fine well the police had not taken her seriously enough to look for him. She had images of him lying at a roadside being hurt or captured by a mafia gang, waiting to be tortured.

The longer time went on, the bigger the fear grew in her mind. We headed back towards the square, where the taxi had dropped us off to find another, Belinda walked behind me all the way. She was so deflated; her energy was lost. We stood for a while in the busy square, unable to get a taxi. A local man pointed us to a bus station across the square and advised us that this would be much quicker than waiting for a taxi at that time of day.

Belinda spoke very little as we waited for the bus but carried on crying into numerous tissues she took from her purse like a magician's hat. I looked at her as we sat on the bus with her head leaned against the window, she looked old as the sun gleamed down onto her face, exposing every line of her skin. A realization that she was head-over-heels in love, made me feel sick to the pit of my stomach. I knew the hurt of the deception that she was going to have to face.

The bus stopped for a while as the driver left his seat and walked across the road to have a cigarette. He stood with another man drinking black tea as he enjoyed his break. Looking around, I could recognize the area where we had stayed on the first night.

"Let's get off here and we can go get some food at that little restaurant, and you can pretend to be a food critic again. You never know we may get that free meal they promised?" I asked.
Belinda didn't look too pleased with my suggestion as she turned to me with a look of disgust saying, "Funnily enough, knowing my fiancé is missing, I can't face a thing to eat."

I was quietly pleased that she had down-graded him from her husband to her fiancé and took the initiative to state that we were going anyway and left the bus. Belinda reluctantly followed on behind as we looked for the restaurant, we did not have far to walk and the restaurant looked as quaint in daylight as it had in the evening. We sat at one of the small iron tables situated outside, under a flower-covered entrance. A jar of small red flowers adorned the centre of the table, complimenting the dusky pink tablecloth.

"Well, this is lovely," I pointed out, trying to cheer her up.

Belinda ignored my comments as she rummaged through her purse for her sunglasses to hide her eyes which were swollen red from crying, "Lovely," she replied in a sarcastic tone.

I ordered two fruit juices from the waiter, but she quickly changed her order to a large gin. I tried to change the subject away from her worries as I read the menu out loud, trying to tempt her into eating something, the walk to the police station had made me hungry.

"Oh, the beautiful ladies! My very own food critics! I am so pleased you have returned," a voice said from behind my chair. It was the chef from the restaurant we had met on our first visit. He took the menu from my hand saying, "Let me surprise your taste buds," as he clicked his fingers and a young waiter came to his call. "Get these ladies a pink cocktail - they are our special guests so see they have everything they desire."

Within minutes, candles were placed on our table and two large pink cocktails full of fruit arrived. The drinks were shortly followed boards of mezze, all of which tasted divine. Belinda began to relax, and after three cocktails, her mood lifted, slightly. A further large bowl of goat's cheese salad arrived with fresh warm bread. I could barely eat another thing, but it tasted far too nice to leave.

Belinda leaned back in her chair telling the young waiter to pass on her compliments to the chef, describing him as an exceptionally talented and adding that she would be sure to mention him in her next blog.

"Hammett will be pleased to hear that, thank you," the young waiter answered as he cleared away some dishes from our table. We were so full that neither of us felt like we could move as we slumped further into our chairs, sipping the last of our cocktails. The chef re-appeared from the kitchen, removing his apron as he walked towards our table.

"I am so pleased to hear you liked my food, ladies. It is our taster menu and all feedback is very welcome," he said.

He was invited to take a seat by Belinda as she pulled up a chair for him to sit with us. He chatted about his food ideas and his plans for the restaurant. I found myself drawn to his words by the intense passion in his voice. As more and more drinks arrived at our table, the conversation flowed, we talked about our lives and holidays and laughed about things in life. Belinda talked about Temarh and her problems finding him, Hammett listened intensely as she explained how she had been to the police and felt like they had not taken her seriously. Hammett stood to his feet saying, "Give me a minute I might have an idea."

Hammett had been gone for over twenty minutes when he returned to our table smiling like a Cheshire cat. "Your worries are about Temarh are over, my beautiful lady. He is very much alive and well and with his friends on what I think you call a 'stage' night in Istanbul. Our young bar man, Aslan, knows a friend of a friend of his, and they have just looked him up on Facebook. Temarh is there, and on the pictures is very much alive and well."

Belinda's faced turned red with fury as she stood to her feet, throwing her serviette onto the table. "My fiancé is definitely not on a stag night, nor a stage night, as you so foolishly pronounce it, if he were at a party at all, I would know about it. I am sure whoever gave you the information was very much mistaken, and I will thank you to mind your own business." I quickly apologized for Belinda as I packed up our things to follow her as she stropped off in a fast pace towards the main street.

"I am sorry!" Hammett shouted behind us as we left. By the time I reached the main street, Belinda was sat in a taxi waiting for me.

I was furious at her rude behaviour and did not need to say anything as my face spoke a thousand words. Not one single word was actually spoken between us until we arrived at the hotel, when I slammed the shower door shouting "You didn't need to be so rude! Just because you didn't like what he had to say." Belinda did not retaliate, she just sat on the balcony until the early hours and drank gin.

The next day was our last day of our holidays and I felt more than a little relieved. The atmosphere between us was still awful and only polite conversation passed between us.

That morning I stayed around the pool determined that I would go home with a suntan. Belinda did not join me, she wandered around the town and made a return trip to the golf club, but to no avail.

I returned to the room, showered, and packed my things ready to depart. I could not help but feel guilty about the way Belinda had treated Hammett and thinking how nice he had been. I arranged to meet Belinda in the foyer and took a taxi to see Hammett and make my apologies.

Knowing I was running tight on time, I asked the driver to wait while I went into the restaurant. Aslan greeted me from behind the bar and asked if I wanted a table. "I have just called to see Hammett, if he is available? I don't want to bother him if he is busy?" I asked.

Aslan went off to check, and as I stood waiting, I noticed how busy the restaurant was and started to feel that my quest was a little stupid. Aslan returned from the kitchen quickly followed by Hammett. As he walked towards me, I noticed how lovely his smile was. I quickly composed myself and began to offer my apologies for Belinda's behaviour.

Hammett took me to a small table outside and Aslan brought me a drink of juice. I explained that I could not stay and had a car waiting and that I had only returned to apologize and offered to pay for the meal we had had.

Hammett was so very polite and insisted that the meal was on the house. I explained that Belinda was not a food critic and it was just lies that she had made up to make herself sound better. Hammett laughed saying he knew that she was not a critic, and that he was sorry about telling her about Temarh, but that all he had told her was true.

I thanked him once again and stood to leave for my waiting car. Hammett walked with me towards the car and stood holding the door as I climbed into the back seat. He shuffled uncomfortably as he stood, he held the door looking nervous and said
"It has been such a pleasure to meet you, Monica, and I so hope we may meet again sometime? Please tell your friend to take care. Temarh is a young man with things on his mind other than true love, and I fear she may get hurt." With that he closed the car door and stood and waved as we drove away.

Chapter 4

Any sympathy I had for Belinda decreased on our return. She threw her heavyhearted mood onto everyone around her. Despondent, rude and ill-mannered, she made no effort to be social and paraded around like a new widow. Her miserable expression remained steadfast, even as Colin stood loyally at the airport waiting to collect us. He waited eagerly at the glass doors with their little highland terrier wagging his tail with pure joy as he waited to greet her. Belinda who had once loved her dog so much, passed her case to Colin without acknowledging either of them, saying only "Careful! There are breakables in there!"

She walked ahead of him, leaving him to take her case and manage the dog on his lead. She stormed off towards the car, with Colin trailing, as if he where the chauffeur and not her husband.

The whole situation was very uncomfortable, and my pitifully polite conversation did precious little to lift the discomfort. Belinda got to the car and demanded that Colin put the dog in the cage in the back, as she felt she could not tolerate him jumping on her knee with excitement.

"He's just excited to see you. He'll settle down if you pet him," he tried to explain.

Belinda threw a glare at him as she said, "I am aware of how to handle the dog, thank you, Colin. And I am also aware that I am very tired and cannot be fussed with dog hairs all over my clothes. I will thank you not to question me, I did not ask your opinion I gave you a simple instruction, so follow it." The dog also seemed to pick up on her mood quickly and sat quietly in his cage in the rear of the car, no longer seeking or expecting any attention.

At home that evening, my own bed felt like heaven. I showered and made a welcomed cup of tea and sat on my bed with my laptop, looking through emails and eating chocolate. My friend Phil rang, and it was so nice to hear a familiar voice.

"Hello, Hun. It's nice to see you're back in the land of the workers. How was it? I want all the gory details. How is that 'mardy-arsed cow', did she enjoy it?"

I had to take a deep breath and think of where I should start. I suddenly felt an awareness of how pressurized I had felt on holiday and how nice it felt to be away from Belinda and her situation. Phil wanted to know all the details and only interrupted my rendition of the holiday to say "I don't believe it!."

As I finished the story, Phil said "Well, I almost feel sorry for her."

"I feel sorry for Colin – he's going to lose everything, and he has no idea. She is treating him like he has no rights or say in the matter. She is so harsh," I said.

Phil seemed excited by the story and demanded to know more details. "What is his name? I'm going to look him up."

"Who?" I asked.
"Temarh the Amazing, who'd you think?" he answered sarcastically.
I had to think for a second to realize I wasn't even sure of his second name and pointed out to Phil that even in a few days of searching, I knew precious little about him and suspected that Belinda knew even less.

"Just call me Inspector Phil and leave it with me. My years of stalking have taught me many skills." Phil was pleased with his challenge and left the call like a man on a mission.

That night, I slept so well that getting up when the alarm went off needed more energy than I could muster. After snoozing the alarm four times in a row, I gave up and turned it off. This was a bad move, as then I slept late.

I eventually turned into work half an hour after time, and looking less than professional than I should do, with my untamed hair and creased t-shirt that I had hoped would go unnoticed under my jacket. I rushed to my desk and straightened my clothes and rang for Leanne's attention. I turned on the computer and composed myself, as I called again for Leanne. With still no answer, I looked around my office door to see her standing at the photocopier with Dan from human resources. He was the office eye-candy, but sadly loved himself far more than he could ever love anyone else, but Leanne looked hopeful nonetheless.

I raised my voice, "Leanne, can I have my diary please?" I asked.

"It's in your drawer," she answered, in a dulcet tone without turning to face me.

My tone was now more demanding. "My electronic diary - I need you to go through a few things with me, please?" I felt that my tone was enough to assert my authority and headed back to the office to wait for her arrival.

Leanne took her time in finishing her hair flicking and giggle-filled conversation with Dan, and sauntered towards my office, taking a quick pouting 'selfie' as she walked. Refusing to acknowledge her obvious lack of respect I ignored her pace and attitude as if she where a small child demanding attention.

"Now, let's get things sorted. Firstly, why are there no appointments for the Briggs and Lace coffee account? There should be at least three for this month - the deadline is September?"

Leanne sat looking at her mobile phone smiling at the pictures that Dan had obviously just sent her.

"Leanne, could you put that down for a moment and concentrate please?" I asked in a demanding voice. She rolled her eyes and placed her mobile phone down onto the table.
"Now! The Briggs and Lace?" I asked.

"You're not on it anymore. They've given it to Janice Sweeting, the deadline was brought forward, so she went to finalize it all while you were away." She paused for a while and with a smirk on her face took great pleasure asking, "Didn't they tell you?"

I had been working on that contract for months, I had put over and above the hours in. The thoughts of the evenings I wasted schmoozing clients who I could not stand just to get this contract ran through my mind.

Trying not to lose my composure I said, "Of course they did. I'm asking you where they are up to out of interest. I put a lot of time into that account."

Leanne rolled her eyes again, picked up her mobile and stood to her feet. "You are on the brainstorming group for the new dog chew advert. It's on your emails, Janice said it be one for you to get your teeth into." Leanne laughed out loud at her own innuendo as she left the office.

Feeling furious, I was about to tell her to get me a coffee but thought better of it and went to the kitchen myself. I could feel the anger showing in my face as I stood waiting for the kettle to boil. Clive from finance came in to get his almond and soya milk from the fridge which was clearly identified by a sticker with his name on.

"Nice to see you back, Monica," he said, attempting to be friendly.

"I've only been gone a few days, Clive. It was a short break for family reasons, not a round-the-world single-handed sailing trip in an old tin bath."

Clive pursed his lips at me as he sniffed the carton of milk to test its freshness. Clive always looked like life had passed him by. He wore the same clothes every day, a pale blue shirt and a pink tie, which he thought made him look hip. In his mid-fifties, his thinning brown hair was combed over at one side, he looked every inch the henpecked husband. I often wondered how he ever came to meet his wife as his conversation was beyond boring? His wife had never actually been seen, and rumour had it that he wore a wedding ring for pretence and in reality, he lived with his mother. The only picture on his desk was a colourful picture of the flying Scotsman in all its glory, but no trace of the illusive 'Joyce'.

The kettle came to the boil and I started to make my coffee.

"Janice did well with the contract, I hear?"

"Did she, Clive? I don't really know I'm busy on other things," I answered flippantly.

In a monotone voice he replied, "I heard you've been put on the dog chew contract not much glory there."

I suddenly saw another side to Clive - his nasty streak had raised its ugly face.

"How is Joyce keeping these days?" I asked. Clive did not answer but just mumbled to himself as he walked away with his milk carton and a rinsed clean glass.

The end of my day could not come quick enough, so at three-thirty I made my excuses to leave early and decided to cabin myself up at home and eat my body weight in chocolate.

That evening, the sight of Phil at my door with two large bottles of wine was a welcome sight. Evenings with Phil comprised of loungewear, gossip, food and wine. Lounging at home helped when the wine became too much, as I could just fall straight into bed comfortably with minimal effort, with or without my jim-jams with Rue my dog to keep me company.

Phil began to pour the wine. "Well, just call me 'Monsieur Cousteau' because I have uncovered quite a bit about our Turkish friend."
"Really? How the hell did you do that, because we looked and only found holiday photographs?"

Phil looked at me, pausing for a second as he looked up from his laptop. "We? Who might the proverbial 'we' be? Is there something I should know?"

I hated how perceptive he was at times - he often seemed to know me better than I knew myself.

I stuttered an answer, "Hammett looked mostly, but me and Belinda tried to find any information we could but got nothing."

Phil raised his eyebrows as he said, "Hammett! Mmmm…. Well, you named the puppy. Tell me more about Hammett, my dear," he said sarcastically as if he were my psychologist.

Defensively, I blurted out "There's nothing to tell! He's just someone we became friends with. He worked in a local restaurant near where we stayed. Well, actually it wasn't local, but it was somewhere we went to and liked."

Phil looked at me and said nothing.

"Don't give me that look – there's nothing to tell!" I insisted.

Phil paused and gave me that look again saying, "I never said there was."

Trying to quickly change the subject, I asked him about what information he had found.

"Swiftly moving on then," he said sarcastically, "Temarh, or Tom as he is otherwise known, is practically a social butterfly. He's a busy boy on Tinder, plus a few other more selective sites. Belinda has bagged herself a looker, I have to give her that. His photographs are definitely eye candy. He is very well travelled and educated is our boy, and he's not shy when comes to being seen with sugar mammy," Phil said smugly, proud of his detective skills.

"Oh, no, please? She's going to be completely broken. Show me - I need to see it for myself," I said as I turned the screen to my direction.

There he was, as large as life, very much the poser. Pictures appeared by the dozen, all in different places and all showing him enjoying the finer pleasures of life. Phil returned the screen towards him and typed a few keys then turned it back to me saying, "Here he is again, but this is Tom!" There he was posing on a yacht, but this time under a completely different name with his relationship status as 'it's complicated.' I flicked through the pictures and updates I could hardly believe my eyes.

"Small wonder you couldn't find him going by his status, he's a busy boy all week. His abductors must have given him a free holiday with the boys, allowing him to pose with the odd bikini-clad beauty," Phil held his stomach as he laughed.

"I almost feel sorry for Belinda, but to be honest she must be unhinged, because this farce of a relationship is laughable. If you scroll further down, it was only two weeks ago when he was in a relationship with a stunning young brunette called Elise, and she is a far cry from Belinda."

He scrolled down to reveal a picture of a beautiful longhaired girl with a figure to die for. They stood together cuddling under a 'wishing tree' with their wish ribbon ready to hang on their chosen branch. The thought of how hurt Belinda would be made me feel devastated for her, my sympathy for her regrew. My mind spun with different ways to break the news to her, none of which seemed like a good option. I thought that night that I would ring her, but then I wondered if Colin would hear, or if night time was the best time to deliver some bad news. I decided to sleep on it and ring her first thing in the morning.

The next morning, I was late as usual and left for work in a rush. I grabbed a banana on my way out of the house, slightly praising myself for eating healthily and deciding that this was the start of a new healthier me.

I called at the coffee shop drive-thru on my way to work, as figured that I was late anyway, so twenty more minutes would not matter. As I shouted through the drive-thru window, "Please can I have coconut milk latté?" to the barista who was ignoring me as he talked into his head set.

My mobile phone rang - it was Belinda sounding very excited and full of life. I tried to answer her as the barista came back to the window asking what I had shouted.

"Coconut milk latté please? I wasn't sure if you had heard me saying that I would prefer coconut milk?"

I could hear Belinda on the phone asking what I was talking about. I tried to shout across the car to explain that I was at the drive-thru, but she hung up before I could explain. Within seconds she had sent me a text saying that she could not really talk now but she would call at my house later as she had some news for me.

I drove on with my coffee, feeling relieved at the thought that she may already know what I had already found out, and that I would not have to be the bearer of bad news.

As the morning wore on, I thought of ways that I could be her shoulder to cry on and googled spa days, thinking a relaxing day might help to kick start mending her emotions.

Leanne entered my office without knocking, throwing down four letters onto my already messy desk.

"Thank you, Leanne, but do remember to knock in future," I said sternly.

"Big Griff wants to see you in his office asap!" she snapped as she left.

Big Griff was my boss. His name was actually Griffyn Sevelle - a self-made millionaire and something of a celebrity in the advertising industry. They called him 'big Griff' due to his stature. He had been a successful rugby player in his younger days for his home team in Wales and still looked the part. He had a dark complexion which was inherited from his Spanish mother's roots, and he had deep brown eyes from his father. He had impeccable dress sense and always looked every bit the successful businessman, even in his sport's wear, that he would often change into as he left the office when off to play badminton.

I walked towards Griffyn's office knowing fine well being called there was never good. His office had glass walls made especially for him, as he said it made him feel more part of the team and an approachable boss. The truth was far from that, as most of the time he had the blinds pulled down for privacy. As I walked toward his office I could see Janice Sweeting sat at the side of his desk laughing and swaying her hair as she chatted to him like a love-struck teenager. Griffyn saw me walk towards the door and waved his hand for me to come straight in. Janice was holding a red and yellow necktie that she had bought him from her holidays.

"Come in and take a seat. Join in the joke it's not a private one. Look what Janice has picked up for me from Disney World! One for Christmas day, I think," Griffyn said as he swiftly put it into his drawer.

Janice giggled and said, "Well, I saw it and thought of you with it being Griff," then giggled again as if she had been immensely funny. My face didn't change. My mother would have described my look as 'miserable as sin.'

"Did you want me for something, Griff?" I asked, as if I were short of time and they were wasting what little I had.

"I did, Mon. Do come and sit so we can talk. I just wanted to keep you up to speed with the Briggs and Lace contract. As you will be aware, Janice kindly stepped in at the last minute to support you while you were away on your family emergency." Janice giggled again. I said nothing. It felt like my safe strategy at that moment.

Griff went on. "Now, I won't ask what the emergency was, Monica, because I trust you to be honest with me. Despite this however, there are rumours going around the office that you have, in fact, been sunning yourself on a short break. In my position, I do not have the time or the inclination to listen to rumours so we'll say no more on that matter. This does, however, shed light on the level of commitment required for a contract as large as the Briggs and Lace one - a contract worth too much money to slack on. Thankfully, we had Janice, who was ready and willing to hit the ground running when you were predisposed. The clients loved her, which is a 'win-win' situation. I can't help feeling though, we may have dodged a curveball there, and need to step-up a notch, as we have plenty of competitors just waiting for us to fail - to swoop in and take over. So, with all this in mind, I've asked Janice to kindly take the lead on this contract, leaving you some space to take care of your family business. Janice has kindly accepted the challenge and said she would be more than happy for you to chip in with any comments from time to time. Isn't that right, Janice?"

Janice sat upright from her slumped position like a slutty schoolgirl, desperate to find the right answer. "Yes, that's correct. Any help will be gratefully received," she said as she giggled again.

I could hardly think of a civil word to say. I had worked tirelessly on that contract for months. I could say goodbye to my bonus which I was counting on to relieve some financial pressures. I merely smiled and got up to leave, trying my hardest to hold in my tears and a mouth full of obscenities.

Griff shouted as I went to close the door, "Just before I forget, I've asked Leanne to pick up some work from Janice just to take the pressure off a little - keeps her load manageable. I said I was sure you wouldn't mind sharing her for a while. Also, I'm loving the ideas on the 'Big Chew' dog campaign - keep them coming!"

 I sat back at my desk and watched Janice as she practically floated across the office with joy. "I love that nail varnish, Leanne, you do choose the nicest colours. Shall we have a coffee?" Leanne gushed and stood to make the coffee saying, "Yes, I'll make - it I know how you like it."

I sat slumped at my desk like a deflated balloon. I had never really taken much notice of Janice before now, and suddenly she had become public enemy number one. Janice had always been the office cry-baby and seemed to be going through her divorce for at least five years. And yet now she was suddenly every inch the Machiavellian business woman. She cried so much, that at Christmas someone bought her a personalized cover for her tissue box. Everyone in the office knew the sordid details of her husband Raymond's affair. It was common knowledge that she had spent years on fertility treatment, only to be told they could not try again because she was too old. Raymond had left her for a woman ten year his junior and then the new bit on the side fell pregnant, and they could no longer keep their relationship secret. Raymond had left her financially sound, but emotionally broken. Tracey from supplies had heard a rumour, that Janice had hired a life coach and her life had taken on a new perspective. Gone were the chintzy dresses and clumpy shoes and in came the sharp suits, crisp shirts and cha-cha heels.

That afternoon I took root at my desk feeling overwhelmingly sorry for myself. I tried to ring Phil to cheer myself up, but even his telephone went to voicemail.

I left work early that day, unable to muster any enthusiasm for dog chews. The traffic getting home was exactly as I would have expected for the mood of the day – slow, sweaty and bloody miserable. I managed to hit every traffic light as it turned red, and I drove behind every learner driver, dumper truck and tractor.

As I pulled onto my drive, I was surprised to see Belinda sat in the summer chair in my garden, in front of the window, smoking a cigarette. As I climbed out of the car, she stubbed out her cigarette into my geraniums much to my displeasure.

"Don't mind my plants, will you?" I said sarcastically as I walked into the garden.

"Don't be a grumpy, Monica. I am the bearer of good news," Belinda said beaming with joy.

I unlocked the door, "Oh good! I could do with some good news today."

Belinda shuffled passed me in the passageway saying, "Temarh has been in touch, and he's fine! I'm so relieved - I was practically out of my mind with worry."

"That's good of him, considering you flew all that way to see him and then he never bothered to show up," I answered flippantly, much to Belinda's disappointment.

"Actually, Monica, he was desperately sorry when he got in touch. He was with his sick mother and they live in the countryside. There was no way he could leave his father on his own to care for his mother or to get away from the house to get a signal."

I looked at Belinda lost for words that she actually believed this story.

"Jackanory springs to mind," I said as I headed for the kettle for some cure-all tea.

"No tea for me thanks – I've got to go. I just wanted to give you the good news," Belinda was no longer smiling. She paused for a minute as if to take stock of what she wanted to say.
"Monica, you are my best friend and I love you, but Temarh is the love of my life, and you either support me or there can be no friendship between us. He has given up so much for me - he is an honest, loving, passionate man, and I am so lucky that we found each other. You know how hard good chemistry is to find, so when you find it you have to treasure it. He makes me feel like the only woman in the world, please just give him a chance?"

"There's something I have to tell you Belinda, and I am so sorry to be the one to ruin your dreams, but Temarh is playing you for a fool. He isn't the man you think he is, he is a liar and cheat. Phil found him on a dating website and he uses different profiles. He was active on there all of the time we were looking for him. He is telling you what he thinks you want to hear."

Belinda picked up her bag and coat to leave. "Well, if Phil the 'bitter' gay says it then it must be true! Monica, I never had you down as being so shallow, but where Phil is concerned, you are the biggest fool of us all. Temarh has told me about his social media sites and they are old sites that he no longer uses. Unlike you, he doesn't feel the need to expose his full life on social media. Have you ever stopped in your detective work to think he is too busy caring for his family and studying, to bother updating sites he no longer needs or cares about? Anything you think you have seen is simply a ghost of his past. This is a new chapter in our lives, and I will be taking that chance regardless of your Victorian views."

Belinda stormed out f the house slamming the door as she left.
I felt the day could get no worse and took a bottle of wine in the bath to keep me company in my despair.

Days went by and I heard nothing more from Belinda. I was getting used to no longer being important in the office and decided to enjoy the reduced pressure of work.

Redecorating my house was my idea of sorting out the clutter from my emotional life. I started with my kitchen, which had been looking a little shabby of late. After painting two walls a fresh shade of blue, I cleaned the brushes in a bucket at the sink. Rue started to bark furiously at the front door. I had not heard anyone knock or press the bell, so I assumed it must be someone passing by and shouted Rue to settle down. Rue's barking got louder, so I dried my hands to go and see what was causing Rue to be so upset.

I was suddenly startled by a large thud coming from the passageway. Rue and I both yelped as the door was rammed open. Colin fell headlong into the doorway, Rue grunted and growled, gnarling at his feet. My heart was racing. My face flushed. Panic. What the…? I tried to compose myself. I was in shock. Fully drunk, Colin tried to brush Rue away with a sweep of his hand, only for her to gnash out at him.

Colin was so drunk he could hardly stand, even with my assistance. I managed to get him sat in an upright position and eventually got him some coffee. He managed to sip a little after lots of encouragement. His eyes were red and swollen and he mumbled nonsense. He was totally incoherent. I asked him what was wrong but he only gurgled an answer as he drooled into his coffee. I called Belinda on her mobile but got no reply, even after sending her a text asking her to call me urgently.

After twenty minutes, I managed to get Colin to his feet and into the living room and onto the sofa. There he drooped to a heap in an over-emotional drunken stupor. He limply pulled out a torn envelope from his pocket, which consisted of three sheets of official looking papers. "That's it – it's final. All our future plans - everything lost." I opened the letter it was the 'decree nisi', evidenced in black and white - the end of their marriage.

Between his tears and his muttering, he managed to tell me that Belinda had applied for a divorce some months ago, but he had thought she would change her mind and stay with him. She hadn't, and the divorce had gone through and been finalized. He had hoped that her wish for divorce had come from some 'mid-life crisis.' He felt that by going along with her wishes she would eventually change her mind, and life would go back to normal.

He wailed some more as he told me he was worried about her, and how she had been acting strangely. He was aware that she was no longer interested in their little dog, nor did she visit her mother. She had even sold the time-share they had had for years. "She would never do that - she loved Greece - we were going to retire there. We've been going there for years." My heart broke for him as he put his case forward as being a good husband and loving her, while simultaneously apologizing for his failings. He begged me to help her to come to her senses, saying he worried about her more and more each day.

I went into the kitchen to make him another coffee but got back to find him fast asleep and snoring. I took a blanket from the cupboard and covered him as he slept. I sent another text to Belinda telling her he was at my house, and not to worry, but I was pretty sure she did not care how or where he was.

I went to bed and messaged Phil telling him all about Colin and how bad I felt for him. His reply was swift and to the point.

SHE DOESN'T LOVE ANYONE BUT HERSELF. HE HAS HAD A LUCKY ESCAPE. MARK MY WORDS; THIS WILL BE THE BEST THING THAT EVER HAPPENED TO HIM.
HE WILL LOOK BACK ON THIS DAY AND WONDER WHY THE HELL HE EVER CRIED. WHEN HE LOOKS BACK HE WILL HAVE TEARS OF JOY THAT HE GOT RID OF HER.

I awoke that morning to find Colin had gone and the blanket folded neatly on the arm of the sofa. I had a blunt text from Belinda, saying that she did not care and not to bother her again. I showed the text to Phil during coffee in the canteen that morning.

"Cheeky cow! It's her husband how dare she? She's a selfish woman and good things don't happen to bad people, so basically, she's fucked. You watch Hinny, karma is a bitch." Phil stood to his feet reminding me he had to go because he actually had a life. He had met someone, but was giving away very little information about him, which led me to think it may actually be serious. Or else, embarrassing.

"Don't forget it's salsa class tomorrow, pick you up at six? Got my Cuban heels at the ready," and with that he floated away, graciously pirouetting as he left the room, giggling to himself.

I had forgotten all about salsa class but had promised to go at the same time that I had decided to decorate my home and change my life. These plans always seemed a good idea at the time. Fuelled by a bottle of wine and heaps of enthusiasm, they never seemed so good in the cold light of day. I had mentally shelved the idea of salsa and keep fit classes, along with the many books on how to stay positive, all bought with good intentions but no real objectives. As I sat back at my desk, I decided that positivity was the goal for the day, and I was not only going to go to salsa but was determined to enjoy it, too.

I opened my inbox and decided to tackle the backlog of five hundred emails that I had been avoiding for weeks. The task proved to be too large, so I decided to break them down into three categories - 'Urgent', 'Can be done later' and 'Can't be arsed'. Pretty much all them went into the 'Can't be arsed' category. Pleased with myself for clearing up that mess, I made a coffee (no longer having the luxury of Leanne to bring beverages) and tackled the 'Urgent' list.

An email from Leanne popped up saying simply, YOU SENT ME THIS TO DO CORRECTIONS BUT NONE OF IT MAKES SENSE SO I CANT.

My immediate response was how dare she be so impertinent only to read the email and not be able to make sense of what I had written? Excruciatingly, I had written 'Hammett' instead of the word 'having' in the body of the email and had not even realized. I started to feel a bit out of sync with myself. Never before had I felt as though I had let things in my life get so out of control. I needed to get a grip on life, if not at home, then definitely at work.

Things were starting to get on top of me. I no longer felt confident or grounded, but uneasy and directionless. The last time I had felt this bad was during my divorce, and that was over a decade ago.

My divorce had been pretty amicable and straightforward as divorces go. Jake had left me financially comfortable and always supported me since. He gave no argument when it was time to send Lilly to university and remained the doting father to her. I looked at the photograph of Lilly on my desk, which showed her smiling on holiday. I sent her a text asking how things were, and to ring if she could chat, but received a swift reply of FINE MUM. BUSY AT THE MIN SPEAK SOON X. Feeling totally deflated and unloved, I headed off to the High Street to find something to wear for salsa. Retail therapy was always good for the soul.

I felt excited by the time I set off to class with my new purchase of a red, short, flared dress with matching heels. I had nearly bought a red rah-rah skirt but thought better of it when I saw the skinny sales assistant snigger to her friend.

I felt very much the part of a salsa dancer. Phil was waiting for me at the door as I arrived; telling me to hurry as we were late and the others had already gone in and taken their positions. I had expected the class to be held in a dusty church hall but was pleasantly surprised to see a real salsa club. The room had a circle of small round tables that enclosed the dance floor. The tables where covered in dark velvet cloths which matched the heavy velvet drapes that dressed the windows and the fire exit. The bar was small and stood in the corner, as if it were an insignificant part of the club. Tiffany lamps stood on the tables providing a mood light that enhanced the ambiance.

"This place is great, isn't it?" Phil asked.

"It's fabulous - I didn't even know it existed," I answered.

"Stick with me and you will go places," Phil said laughing.

There was a small empty stage at the front of the room with band instruments set up to play. I got quite excited at the thought of a real band playing. I could practically envisage myself as a professional salsa dancer wowing people with my dancing skills. That dream was abruptly halted as the instructor walked in. The dancing teacher carried an oversized portable CD player. He looked nothing like the Latino American teacher I had imagined. He was in his mid-fifties with balding grey hair and stood about five-foot-five, even in his Cuban heels. Despite his demure stature, he confidently clapped his hands turned on the music and strutted to the middle of the floor demanding our attention.

"Ladies, ladies, let's get started. Sophie, let's start?" he said as he held out his hand to be joined by a slim, beautiful, dark-haired girl who towered him by over a foot. We stood and watched in awe as they began to dance with expertise, enthusiasm and hips to die for. This little man swung her around on the dance floor as if he was six foot tall. They seemed to know each other's moves, dancing in complete synchronicity, as they glided across the floor making every complex move look simple.

"Why can't I look like her? Her arse looks like a ripe peach. Mine looks like two out-of-date butternut squashes in a bag, these days."

"Mine too, sadly," Phil replied.

We both sat staring at the performance in silence, watching her arse and thinking of our own.

"How old do you reckon she is, Phil?" I asked.

"Sophie? She looks younger than her years - she is in her late thirties, I would think, but she doesn't look a day over twenty-five, does she? You should see her social media – it's a life we can only dream of. That's what comes of having no children- you get to keep your figure.
"And your dignity and your life," I added.

"We play the cards we are dealt with Hinny. It's just some are better players or get dealt a better hand than others."

I nodded in agreement; as Phil went on to tell me Sophie was a yoga instructor who had been doing some relaxation sessions at Watson and Watson law firm recently. He had found out about the classes through a friend who worked there.

"I wonder if Jake knows her. He does lots of shared contract work there, doesn't he? I can't imagine he has much to do with yoga though, to be honest. He is more interested in throwing beer down his neck than finding his Zen."

"You must be joking - I imagine a few of them are turning to relaxation, what with her taking the classes. I bet they're all stripping off their suits and donning their Lycra bodysuits in their droves," Phil sniggered at his own answer.

We were ordered to stand to our feet and were shown some simple turning moves.

"Concentrate on the hips! Let's see them hips swing, ladies. It's all in the swing," the teacher said as he walked around observing our arses. Phil seemed to be taking it very seriously and was not fazed as we were told to do three steps back and turn moves, then swap partners until the full class had all swapped with each other at least once. I felt really uncomfortable and could not seem to get a rhythm, whereas Phil was gliding from dancer to dancer with ease. As we paired up again, I complimented Phil on his skill, saying he looked like a natural.

"I want to be good at this – I'm going to impress Warren," he said as he spiralled off to another partner.

"Is that your new man?" I asked as we passed again swiftly.

"Oh, believe me - he is all man and all mine. I intend to keep this one," he said as he swung of to the other side of the room with a middle-aged grumpy-looking woman with a perm, who swiftly reminded me we were there to dance, not talk. Cow.

Talking between swings, I pointed out that he had kept quiet about Warren, and that I wanted to know more. Partnered-up again, Phil told me that Warren was eleven years his senior and a divorcee from a heterosexual marriage, with two grown-up sons.

"That's not your normal type," I pointed out as Phil hurled me around.

"I don't do normal choices Hinny you should know that, and anyway, I like that he's…well…different."

I took a back step and a turn and asked, "What does he do for a living?"

"He owns a haulage company - a really large one, and I am his first serious relationship since he came out," Phil pointed out proudly.

Although I was happy for Phil, I suddenly felt very inferior, as if my life was falling spectacularly apart, and his had gone from charmed and dramatic to textbook happiness. Without wanting to admit my selfishness, I think the feeling I was experiencing was that of self-interest. Or jealousy. Or hopelessness.

Chapter 5

My big dreams of becoming salsa dance champion of the year ended at that one class, as week after week either Phil or I had an excuse not to go. I gradually saw less and less of Phil, as his relationship with Warren went from strength to strength. Phil had met Warren's two sons and they all got on well, which was a big step for Phil. I decided that due to my obvious lack of a social life, I would join the local gym and get myself fit. In my infinite wisdom, I convinced myself that if I had to pay a monthly fee then it would spur me on to attend. Funds had been pretty low lately with no bonus to lift my financial intake. Jake was becoming increasingly tight with money, often pointing out that Lilly was no longer a child needing support, and that I should manage my money better.

True to my promise, I went to the gym every night after work for over two weeks. I enjoyed the social interaction, as most of my evening conversations were with Rue these days, and dogs are good at cuddles but not advice. I had increased my lengths of the pool from ten in the first week to twenty and felt really pleased with myself. I would finish my swim and sit in the steam room for ten minutes afterwards, convincing myself that it was making me look younger. I had treated myself to a fifties-style bathing costume, which was blue with white polka dots and thought it made my figure look pretty good. I sat in the steam room with my cooling gel eye mask over my eyes, when I heard a voice ask if I minded if he put menthol drops near to the steam inlet. I lifted off my ask mask - I had not realized anyone else had come in.

"Yes, that's fine. It smells really nice - clears the sinuses," I answered. I could not make out his face as the steam in the room was too intense but could clearly see he had a very fit body. I tried to look but without being seen to look. He had sat close to the steam outlet and I could not see. I realized that to leave the steam room I was going to have to walk passed him at a really close range.

From that very moment, the steam seemed to become overpowering. I felt as if I could not breathe. I tried to calm myself by telling myself it was all in my mind, but I could feel a panic attack coming on. My mini breakdown was halted in its tracks by his husky voice as he said, "It's unusually hot in here today, do you think the thermostat could be broken?"

"It's very hot in here! I think maybe *too* hot." I could hear myself babbling. I got up and tried to not walk like my eighty-year-old gran scared of slipping on the wet floor as I passed him. I grabbed my towel and looked in the mirror as I passed on the way to the changing room. I looked like an overcooked lobster with blackened eyes from running mascara.

"Too hot for me, too." I heard a voice behind me say. In my haste to turn to see the source of the voice, I stubbed my toe on the edge of the doorframe to the changing room. I let out the most ear-piercing scream as I attempted to cradle my painful toe, hopping on the wet tiles.

"Let me see I promise I know what I am doing I'm a paramedic. My name is George and very handy at first aid when there is a damsel in distress, or a cute girl with a stubbed toe in need of assistance." Despite my pain, he made me smile as he examined my toe and said that with his x-ray vision he was sure it wasn't broken, and that I was just being slightly over-dramatic.

I managed to compose myself, thanked him with a smile, got dried and changed and forced my fat, swollen toe into my shoe. As I got to my car, I could see George driving out of the car park. I waved and shouted thank you again as he left but was sure he had not heard me.

I looked forward to the gym the next day and had a dim hope that I might see George again. On attending the gym, I took my time in the pool and the steam room and left a little deflated that I had not seen him. As I got to my car, there was a note on my car windscreen, placed under the wiper. It was a hand-written note on a used envelope.

YOU NEED AIR IN YOUR RIGHT-SIDE FRONT TYRE CAREFUL HOW YOU DRIVE UNTIL IT'S FIXED.
FROM YOUR FAVOUIRITE PARAMEDIC
MY NUMBER IS 738973 IF YOU'RE EVER IN NEED OF RESCUING X

I smiled at myself as I folded the envelope and put it into my bag. I had actually been chatted up and it felt like such a long time since anyone had been interested in me. I got home and ran myself a hot bubble bath and contemplated texting George. Two glasses of wine later and despite a disapproving look from Rue, I convinced myself that it was a good idea. I dreaded the thought of waiting for a reply, so I decided to send a text first, then soak in the bath and not check my phone until I got out.

I texted: HI MY FAVOURITE PARAMEDIC HOW ARE YOU ON THIS COLD WET EVENING? I had decided that didn't sound too intense, just in case he decided not to reply. I turned the phone onto silent, and soaked in the bath, thinking that life was maybe not so bad after all. Feeling very relaxed and in my robe, I very casually (as if I didn't really care) checked my phone. Three texts! My heart skipped a beat - he was obviously very keen. With a towel wrapped around my wet hair I jumped on the bed to read.

Text one: HI HOWS THE NOT BROKEN TOE? X
Text two: ARE YOU MAKING ME WAIT SO YOU DON'T LOOK TO KEEN SEX KITTEN?

I had to take a second look - who in the hell says 'sex kitten' these days?

Text three: LETS CUT TO THE CHASE MY WIFE BORES ME TO DEATH AND I THINK YOU LOOK LIKE FUN SO HOW ABOUT BEING MY BIT ON THE SIDE AND I WILL SHOW YOU HOW IT FEELS TO BE A SPOILED WOMAN X

My heart sank. The one man I had the slightest hopes for in a long time was a full-on idiot. Words failed me as another text came through. I could hardly bring myself to look at it.

Text four: WOULD YOU LIKE A DICK PIC?

I threw the phone down onto the bed, furious that I could have even been remotely interested in such a buffoon. I picked it up again, and in a rage typed FUCK OFF. He merely answered YOUR LOSS, which infuriated me even more.

Mad at myself as much as with him, I stormed around the bedroom and dressed in the fluffiest pyjamas I could find, as I needed comforting. I lay in bed and about to start a new novel, in an attempt to take me away from real life for a while, when the telephone rang. I noticed the number was withheld and my immediate thought was George. Prepared to give him hell I answered the phone with an onslaught of insults until I was stopped in my verbal wrath by a young girl's voice saying, "Sorry, but is this Monica?"

In my embarrassment I apologized profusely and asked who was calling.

"I am really sorry to bother you, I'm Grace, Belinda's daughter. I know we haven't spoken for a while and it is little late in the night, but I am desperately worried about Mum."

Grace lived in London. She had moved there after meeting her husband who was a stockbroker. He was rather high up in his industry and Grace was a successful wallpaper designer. She had never had the best relationship with her mother but kept in touch with her father. I listened to her as she poured her heart out to me, concerned that her mum was in trouble. She told me how Belinda's bank account was empty and that she had cut off all ties with her friends. Things in the home had been sold without her father's knowledge, and Colin had, in fact, been staying with Grace for a number of months. Their little dog had been rehomed with an aunt - Belinda intimating she had developed an allergy to dogs and could no longer keep him. She had heard rumours that her mum had been regularly travelling to Turkey and assumed there was another man involved. "You know, me and Mum will never see eye to eye on anything, but I'm scared she's being conned. You read so many stories about these things. She is not answering any calls or emails. Please, Monica, if you know anything or can help, please, I would be so grateful? Dad is worried sick."

We talked for a while, and although I did not dare to tell her all that I knew, I said that I would check with work and see if I could take a few days and go over to Turkey to see her. Grace offered to pay for my trip and stay there for a while, which I was secretly grateful for, as funds had become so tight lately.

We finished the conversation with a promise that if I could have holidays agreed with work, that I would go, but part of me was not sure that would happen.

Deciding that all men where a waste of time, I made a decision to concentrate on getting my career back on track and give Janice Sweeting a taste of her own medicine. I arrived at work early each morning and stayed until late. I continued to be given the small contracts, but I made them the best I could. I pulled out all stops, using all of my contacts in the advertising industry. I felt pretty satisfied with myself. After a few weeks, I received a random email from Griff saying, "Well done on the body cream ad. I think you're back in the game."

Life seemed to taking a turn for the better at long last. I was looking forward to Lilly coming home from university for summer break; it had been so long since I had seen her. Jake had even been really friendly on the odd time our paths crossed, and we arranged a family meal for when Lilly got home.

I asked Phil and Warren to join us for the meal. I thought it would be a good chance to get to know Warren, and Phil was so much like family and had known Lilly since she was a young girl.

The week seemed to fly by so quickly before I was even ready. I found myself running around changing Lilly's bedding and refreshing her room in-between getting ready for the meal. We had arranged to meet in Lilly's favourite restaurant Le Rosal, an Italian eatery that had been passed through the generations, with each chef being as good as the last. Over the years we had celebrated numerous special occasions there - from births to exam passes. It held many good memories for me, I looked forward to going. I had not eaten since early dinnertime and was really hungry and knew the menu off by heart and had already decided what I was going to choose.

I loved the welcoming feeling of the entrance to the restaurant, with its low glow candles and over-hanging purple silk wisteria which crowded the doorway. The tables were covered in the same red and white gingham tablecloths that had adorned the tables for years, and somehow looked better with time. Small, fat bottles stood beautifully in the centre of each table, housing small white fresh flowers that seemed to glow in the light of the candles, which burned away in small glasses on each table.

"Welcome, Miss Monica!" a friendly voice said. Roberto, the owner, walked towards me, kissing me on both cheeks.

"Get out of the way you foolish old man!" His wife, Clara, shuffled him away from me, apologizing for his behaviour, explaining that he went giddy at the sight of a beautiful woman.

"What can I do? I married the old fool and now no-one else will have him. But he is useful at chopping onions," she giggled at her own joke as she took my coat.

"Your family is all here. Lilly is growing into a very beautiful young woman - you should be very proud."

I could see them all across the room - sitting around a round table. I could see Lilly laughing at something her father said, and Clara was right - she had gone away a teenager and came back a beautiful young woman. I walked towards the table to greet everyone, and Lilly stood and ran to hug me. Jake stood to his feet and introduced a young lady next to him.
"I hope you don't mind, but I have brought Sophie tonight. I thought it was about time we all met and this was a good a time as any." Jake stood to one side to reveal Sophie, who nervously stood behind him and uncomfortably said, "Hi!"

Phil looked at me across the table, knowing fine well what I was thinking. Sophie was 'peach butt' Sophie from salsa. The thought that she must be ten years Jake's junior, flashed through my mind and thankfully I hesitated before I uttered anything. She looked even more stunning than she had in class. Her eyelashes looked like she had a camel somewhere in her ancestry. They enclosed the most enormous brown sparkling eyes I had ever seen. Her skin was like silk and her figure was flawless.

"Sit down, Monica - this is Warren." Phil introduced a very handsome bearded man to his left. Warren stood to his feet to greet me, "At last we meet. I have heard so much about you from Phil and all of it good. It is so nice to meet the important people in his life." Phil looked up at Warren and smiled as he took hold of his hand in a gesture of thankful support.

"Well, let's sit down. I'm hungry - I don't know about all of you?" I said as I sat in my seat.
"I hope you don't mind, Mum, but we ordered for you as you are a little late, and Jake and Sophie have to leave early to travel down to Devon," Lilly said apologetically.

Feeling slightly uncomfortable with that, and not wanting to show it, I agreed that that was fine, secretly furious that I was not going to get what I had planned. Thankful for the first glass of wine to relax the mood, I drank it quickly and snacked on bread sticks as the conversation continued.

Despite the uncomfortable start, I actually enjoyed the company. Warren was so friendly and funny I felt my jaw practically ache from laughing. The wine poured, and as the next bottle arrived at our table it was accompanied by champagne flutes on a tray.

"Are we celebrating you home coming, Lilly?" I asked.

Jake stood to his feet to make a speech, saying "Actually this is on me, as there are a couple of things to celebrate around this table tonight." I felt a knot of nervous tension rise up from the pit of my stomach.

"Well, firstly I would like to thank Monica for getting us all together here for this lovely meal. Secondly, I want to say big congratulations to our beautiful daughter Lilly, who today received the news that she has been accepted for an internship in New York this summer. Thirdly, as if that was not enough for everyone, I would like to thank Sophie for accepting my proposal of marriage. I know this is the first time some of you have met, but I can assure you this is not a rash decision, and I know she will be a part of our lovely family. With all that said, would you all raise a glass to us all and a happy future?"

I felt like a fat dog had laid on my chest, I could not breathe. No words came to mind, and I found myself raising my glass to announcements that had just shaken my world. The main course arrived, and I excused myself to the restroom, swiftly followed by Phil, who advised me not to hang myself on the toilet door as it probably would not hold my weight. I bounded between what I would do without Lilly and how the hell my ex-husband had managed to become engaged to the salsa dancer.

"Just breathe deeply Hinny and drink more wine. We can talk later. Get this meal over and be the bigger person – it's all good news, really. It just doesn't feel like that right now," Phil cuddled me in in his own non-tactile way.

Before deserts had arrived, Jake and Sophie had made their excuses and left. Cuddling as they walked out of the door, I watched Jake hold her coat and place it around her shoulders like a true gentleman. Lilly saw my glance and said, "People change, Mum. Dad has changed and for the better. Sophie is really nice and she brings out the best out in him."

In my head I thought 'bully for your fucking father,' but I held my tongue and merely agreed with her by acknowledgement of a nod and a smile.

Shortly after, Phil and Warren made their excuse and left. Phil whispered in my ear as he left, "Warren has paid the bill - don't worry, he can afford it and it goes on the company accounts. I know you're on the bones of your arse financially, so we'll say no more about it. Goodnight, sweetie." He turned to Lilly, "Have a great time in the U S of A - give my love to Trump and bag yourself a nice rich cowboy. Keep in touch, my love," and he kissed her on the cheek.

Lilly was to leave early the next day, but we drank coffee and chatted until late into the early hours. As well as the overwhelming feeling that I was going to miss her, I found myself excited for her future. She had left by the time I woke up the next morning, leaving me a note saying she did not want any sad goodbyes and that she would ring every step of her journey.

I went into work heavy-hearted that morning. My not-so-healthy breakfast consisted of a chocolate bar from the vending machine and a full fat milky coffee with two sugars. I sat slumped at my desk with no intentions of doing any meaningful work; I was far too busy wallowing in self-pity. Leanne was nowhere to be seen and her telephone rang off the hook. Janice trotted passed my office giving me a sideward glance and saying, "Chow." I could not muster any energy to acknowledge her presence, so I pretended not to have seen her. Suddenly the quiet office was invaded by a very loud Leanne, followed by the staff from finance holding balloons shouting congratulations and a cake. "Surprise!" Janice stood to her feet thanking them all and asking how they knew, as she was sure it was not common knowledge yet.

"What isn't common knowledge yet?" I asked standing in the doorway of my office as if I were only half interested.

Leanne blurted out with joy that Janice had been promoted to Associate Director, a post that I had been working towards for years. Alison from human resources came in with yet another balloon, "Congratulations! It is so well deserved! That Briggs & Lace was a big fish to catch - you worked so hard, well done you." This was the straw that broke the camel's back. I could no longer contain my anger and bitterness. I stormed from my office towards her desk and saw Alison take a sharp intake of breath, as if I were charging on horseback with a spear.

"Well earned, my arse! I sweated blood and tears over that contract, and you stole it from under me. Well fuck you and fuck this place!" I stormed back to my desk, picked up my bag and stormed to the lift. As a childish parting shot, I shouted," By the fucking way, balloons hurt wildlife!" I don't know why I would have thought or said that and felt ashamed of it. The lift doors took seemingly hours to close as the full office stared at me. I heard Clive comment that I had 'lost it' just as the doors closed and the lift started moving.

I had no idea what I was going to do, so I kept on walking, in the hope of calming myself down and finding it had all been a bad dream. I walked to the park and sat by the pond. The ducks started to waddle towards my seat, so I dug through my bag and found a low-calorie biscuit in the bottom, which I broke up and threw to them. A few more ducks noted my generosity and swam over to join their friends. They took one taste of the biscuit and left it, swimming off in disgust.

Tears streamed down my face I had even been rejected by the local ducks. My telephone rang. It was Phil, the news of my outburst had spread around the office faster than wild fires.
"What the hell was the balloons thing all about?" he asked disbelievingly.

"I don't know. I just saw somewhere on Instagram the other day about 'balloons don't go to heaven, they go in into the sea' and it stuck in my mind. How could they promote her, Phil? That was to be my job - everyone knew it, too. I'm a laughing stock."

"Well, you are now after that dramatic exit. What the hell where you thinking of? It's a good thing your mortgage-free or you would be in serious trouble right now. Where the hell are you going to work?"

I could not answer him I had no idea what I was going to do. I spent all of that night and the next day moping around the house like a hormonal teenager. Eventually, I decided I needed a break to get my life in some kind of order (again), I called Grace and arranged a flight and accommodation in Turkey in return for rescuing her mum. I felt a heavy burden of guilt, that rescuing Belinda was actually an afterthought, and hoped that my friends were more caring and honest than I was. I lied to my mother about the urgent nature of my trip, as I had to beg her to care for Rue while I was away.

"Oh? Has she gone to be a Jihadi bride? I've read about them in the papers," she asked.

"No, mother she is in Turkey in a holiday resort, not Syria, I'm sure it is an entirely different concept. Will you mind Rue or not? because if not I'll have to put him in the kennels?" Emotional blackmail was one of my strong points.

"What about your work? Haven't you just been away? That will do no good for your career." I cringed at her answer.

"Actually, mother, I am indispensable at work, but they appreciate, that as Belinda's friend this is actually very important and they fully support me."

My father walked into the room at that point, "No-one is indispensable," he said flippantly as he went into the kitchen. He was always right, and on this occasion, it was no different. Unable to give any further argument against my flimsy case, I assumed that they would take care of Rue and left his basket and his food.

As I sat on the flight alone, the thoughts of the karma for being such a selfish cow slightly scared me. I am very much a believer in you get what you give. I justified my guilt as unnecessary, and decided a short holiday was good karma for being robbed of my rightful promotion, and if I helped Belinda in the process, it was a win-win situation.

The flight was uneventful and comfortable, being kept company by three rhubarb gins. My luggage was the first off the carousel and a taxi driver stood waiting for me with a card with my name on it. The sun shone strongly as we drove to the resort, and suddenly life did not seem so heavy and my spirits were lifted.

I arrived at the resort, and much to my pleasure I found the taxi pulling into the drive of the Halm Golf Club and resort. The large gates opened for us, to reveal the beautiful green lawns and bright-coloured bougainvillea that bathed in the glorious sunshine. A concierge opened the car door and my luggage was taken to my room. A lady from reception handed me a telegram. I felt like royalty as I thanked her calmly, taking the envelope as if I was very important and regularly received telegrams. I popped it into my handbag and headed for the lifts. As quickly as the lift doors closed, I tore open the envelope, excited to see who wanted to contact me. It was a lovely message from Grace thanking me for taking the time out to help her with her mum. She appreciated how hard it was to take time out of work to drop everything and just go. She explained how although she did not get on with her mum, it gave her peace of mind knowing that she had such good friends who cared for her. She ended the message saying that she hoped that I enjoyed the hotel, and to take time out for myself while I stayed there, she was happy to pay the bill for anything I needed.

My feelings of guilt returned with a vengeance and prompted me to leave my things and go out and start looking for Belinda straight away. I changed into my shorts and t-shirt and headed off down to reception to make a plan of action. I stood in line waiting to speak to the concierge. The couple in front of me was trying to agree on which day of their holiday they would go scuba diving. I stood for a while, and then decided to take a seat in the nearby sofas in the foyer. As I sat, I marvelled at the atrium across from the entrance. The bright blue sky shone through the windows framing the large green plants. I walked over, deciding to take a look inside. The ceiling was much higher than it had looked from outside and the air in there smelled so fresh and clean. People sat around in the swinging chairs, taking drinks and enjoying their surroundings. I sat for a few moments enjoying the beauty. I texted my mother asking how Rue was and her reply came swiftly.

HE IS DRIVING ME MAD IT IS RAINING AND COLD SO HE HAS NOT BEEN OUT AND YOUR FATHER'S ARTHRITIS IS PLAYING UP x

I could not think of an answer for her and so did not send anything. I ordered a gin and decided to sit for a while and make my plan from there. As I looked out in the gardens, there was hotel staff putting up a gazebo surrounding the doorway with ivy and large white flowers. The waiter brought my drink and commented as I stared at the men at work.

"There is a wedding in the grounds this lunch time," he commented.

The word wedding suddenly jolted me back into the real reason I was getting to enjoy such surroundings.

"Who is getting married?" I asked.

"A couple staying at the hotel, I believe," he said as he placed my drink on the table.

"I know this is a strange question, but would you know if the bride is called Belinda by any chance? She is an irritating older woman with dark hair and plump round the middle?"

The waiter laughed at my description of my friend, but said he was sure that it was not her and thought it might be the daughter of a local businessman. He explained that to be married in the hotel cost tens of thousands and people often had to book years in advance due to its prestigious nature.

I drank my gin and made my way to the concierge to question him on how an amateur sleuth would start to find a missing bride. I tried to make my request sound slightly less bizarre, by explaining I was looking for my friend, and wondered if he could tell me if she had checked into the hotel? He declined to give me the information, politely pointing out that they had a data protection policy and that if she were my friend, why had she not told me where she was staying?

His argument was a fair one, so I tried to explain my predicament and why it was so important that I found her. I told him I was sure she would stay at this hotel, as apart from it being the nicest place to stay, her fiancé actually worked there.

Reminding me that he was unable to give me any client information, he apologized that he was unable to help, but wished me luck in my detective work. I thanked him, and as I walked away from the desk he passed me a note and that had an address written on it. It was the sort of place that someone would go to if they wanted a small intimate wedding in the town and suggested that I should try and get there soon. He was aware there was a wedding be being held there at two in the afternoon. As he handed me the note he said, "Some people do not know that they need to be saved." I thanked him, and now with a feeling of urgency, I ran for a taxi.

The journey took ten minutes. The driver stopped in a large open square which was surrounded by historical-looking buildings, dotted around a small water fountain. The square was full of tourists dipping fingers into the fountain or sitting sipping coffee.

"The Mayor's office is over there to the left," the driver said as he pointed to a small, very scruffy looking building in the very corner of the square, situated next to a mobile drinks stall. I thanked him and headed off to find the Mayor's office. As I walked across the crowded square, I could see Belinda sitting at a cafeteria table next to the drinks stall. Even from a distance I could see that she, too, noticed me, but she made no effort to greet me.

As I got closer, I noticed she was dressed in what looked like a pair of white silk pyjamas. The sheen of the material reflected the hot sun, making it stand out more. As I got closer, I could see she was wearing a tiara of small flowers, which contrasted her sharply-cut dark short hair. She had a white silk scarf draped over her shoulders. She looked like she had gained a lot of weight since I had last seen her. On closer inspection, her eyes looked heavy and her nose was reddened across its bridge. As I walked towards her table, she raised her paper cup as if raising a toast, and said, "Here is to long lost judgmental friends being proved wrong."

I sat in the seat opposite and neither of us spoke for what seemed like a long while. Trying to find the words to start the conversation I stuttered "BBBBBelinda…"

Belinda laughed, "Just for once, the gob-shite is lost for words. Well, let me fill you in. Yes, I am getting married and yes, he does love me, and let me guess - you are only here because Grace sent you?"

I thought of so many responses to her question but decided to say none of them and sat silently. Belinda knew her question was more of a statement and knew the correct response. We both sat quiet again for the next few minutes until Belinda took the higher ground and said, "Well, you're here now and in the nick of time. You can be my maid of honour, even if you are underdressed for the occasion."

With that, the ice was broken and we began to talk. She had been planning the low-key wedding for some months, but the visa and the paperwork had proven more difficult to arrange than she had first thought. She was aware of her family's concerns, but felt they were not justified, and were only fuelled by their ignorance of a love that was able to cross an age gap. She did not care for their concerns and called them small-minded and petty.

I tried in vain to point out they loved and cared for her, but the only love she understood was the love she received from Temarh. She chatted about her outfit, explaining that it was not her first choice of outfit, but had gained so much weight in the past months that it was all she could find to fit her. I didn't ask what had become of the rest of barrage balloon.

I asked where she was staying and she replied the Halm. When I explained that I had looked for her, she proudly said that even if they had given out information, I would never have found her. She was registered under her married name-to-be of Belinda Kaya. I asked if she was sure that this is what she wanted to do, and she quickly and sternly answered that she was surer of this than anything she had ever done in her life. She pointed out that if my intention was to 'put her off' marrying him, then to forget the idea as she wanted nothing more than to be his wife.

Belinda looked at her watch and stood to her feet saying, "Time to get this show on the road."

We walked a few yards round to the side of the building. A scruffy brown door at the top of some stone steps had a plaque saying 'Mayor Travelle'. We stood at the top of the steps for a few moments while Belinda had a cigarette. "He doesn't like me smoking," she said as she drew deeply on it as if it were to be her last. A taxi drew up to the bottom of the steps and Belinda nervously dropped her cigarette to the floor and stamped out the butt. She pulled the scarf from her shoulders and veiled it over her head.

Two young men stepped out from the rear seats of the taxi, both dressed in shorts, t-shirts and flip-flops. I could feel Belinda's excitement build as they walked towards us. The youngest man was fair-haired with blue eyes but very dark skin, which made his eyes look striking. The other was dark haired with chiselled features and very handsome. His pictures had not done him justice. He was easily recognizable as Temarh (or his numerous aliases). The fair-haired man was sniggering loudly has he walked behind Temarh. Belinda did not seem to notice or to care. She completely ignored his presence and at no point took her gaze from Temarh. Temarh hit out at his friend telling him to stop laughing, but he carried on regardless, as if he were unable to stop himself.

We followed them through the scruffy door and waited in a small entrance hall which had a stone floor and plain cream painted walls. After a few moments, we were invited into the Mayor's office by his secretary and told to take a seat. Only three seats where available, so she ran off to find another. Belinda sat near to the desk with Temarh at her right-hand side, and at all times kept her head lowered and her scarf around her head. Very quickly, the secretary came back into the room carrying a chair which she passed to the younger man. He turned it around with the backrest facing the front and sat astride it as if he were riding a horse. He ruffled his hands through his curled hair and said "Fucking hell," as he rubbed his hands across his face then buried his face into his arms rested across the back of the chair. Temarh asked Belinda a question, but so quietly I could not make out what he was saying. It must have had some reference to her scarf as she quickly removed it and held her head higher. As she did so, the younger man burst into a fit of laughter and had to muffle his giggles with his hands.

The situation seemed very uncomfortable as we sat there waiting. The room was small and cluttered with papers and numerous filing cabinets. It looked as if it had been a storage room at some point and things were yet to be collected. The desk surface could not be seen for files and papers colliding with discarded teacups. The only pleasant feature of the office was a large floor to ceiling stained glass window that allowed shards of coloured light to enter the room. The beautiful vista of the window was spoiled by the numerous papers and overflowing ashtrays that littered the window ledge. Behind the desk was a fire surround with cracked beige tiles with a little electric fire in the centre. On top of the mantelpiece stood a framed, hand-drawn child's picture of a stick man with a circle for a stomach and the words 'baba' written underneath. The bars of the fire had numerous circles of burned areas, where cigarettes had been lit. On the far wall hung a very dusty Turkish flag and two pictures of soldiers in full uniform - one of which had slipped from its frame, causing the picture to curl. An old eighties-style telephone stood on the desk half hidden in papers. The ringer had been turned down low and it rang constantly.

After a few moments, a small bald middle-aged man walked in, he wore suit trousers which were held tightly with a belt below his hanging belly. His shirt was tucked in under his belt, the top buttons open exposing a dirty inner collar. As he walked in and sat on his leather swivel chair he said, "Apologies - so very busy. Busy, busy, busy." No sooner had he sat in his chair than he immediately stood to his feet and shook Temarh's hand.

He then held my hand saying, "Pleasure, and is this your mamma?" as he turned to Belinda.

Before I could speak he realized his mistake and said," So sorry - you are the beautiful bride." He then sat back in his chair, unfazed by his faux pas and rifled through the papers on his desk, mumbling to himself. Within a minute, the secretary walked into the room carrying a brown paper file. She placed the file on the desk, then speaking in Turkish, she shouted at the Mayor and waved her hands in the air as she left the room. He took no notice of her remonstrations and lit a cigarette. He placed it into an overfull ashtray as he opened the file. I attempted to move away from the billowing smoke, but very quickly it pervaded the room.

He spoke in Turkish as he quickly flicked through the file and placed two pieces of paper on the table with crosses pointing out the intended signature points. He spoke to Temarh in Turkish, seemingly reciting a paragraph from the afore-mentioned letters. To my surprise, Belinda was asked to recite the same paragraphs and did so fluently (as if well practiced) without fault or stutter. The younger man was then asked to sign but was distracted by his mobile telephone. Temarh seemed agitated by his lack of regard and snapped at him in Turkish. Belinda smiled proudly at her new husband as he took charge and asserted his authority. There was no announcement or congratulations as the Mayor took the two signed sheets and returned with a paper to collect the marriage book. He handed it to Temarh who gestured to Belinda to pick it up and we all left.

As we got to the steps, Temarh said something to his friend, who without saying goodbye to any of us, simply left, ignorantly making a phone call. Belinda beamed with joy as she held onto Temarh's arm in an act of ownership. He seemed unable to hide that he was irritated by her actions and shrugged her arm from his as he walked down the stairs.

Belinda had arranged for a post-wedding celebration meal in a restaurant not far from the square. I was surprised to see the extent of the effort made for our little party. The table was covered in a white linen cloth and dressed with ivy and white roses. Candles lay along the centre of the cloth allowing a glow of orange light to illuminate the table, as the sun lowered into the evening. The staff had written Mr & Mrs in petals on the placemats of the table with flowers surrounding a small wedding cake decorated in white flowers. The table was set for four, but only three us of ate as Temarh's friend had already gone.

To my surprise, Temarh was pleasant and chatty. He ordered food for us and talked about what was best on the menu. He chatted about his studies and his ambitions. He asked about my family and my career, but I declined to admit that I was now unemployed. He showed very little emotion to Belinda but it did not dull her mood - she seemed to smile so much I was sure her jaws hurt.

Despite starting the meal feeling like a spare part, I had to admit I enjoyed the full evening and actually felt that Temarh was a nice person. As the meal drew to an end, we ordered coffee and Belinda talked about her plans for the week. She had booked the bridal suit for the night and had planned a day at the lagoon for them both for the next day. The waiter brought the bill for the meal and handed it to Temarh, which he read and placed on the table. To my disgust I saw Belinda take money from her purse and hand it to Temarh under the table, which he readily took from her. Not a word was said about the exchange as he handed the money to the waiter, then put the left-over change in his pocket.

Belinda looked at him proudly in awe of his new role as 'her man.'

Chapter 6

I left them alone that evening and took a taxi back to my hotel. I had almost forgotten the single purpose for my journey as I looked at my phone and there were three messages from Grace, all three begging for information about her mum. I felt quite ashamed that I had completely forgotten her and her concerns and wondered how the hell I could ring and say, "Hi, everything's OK and I've found her, but on the downside, I have just been to her wedding." I wrote a number of texts all of which I deleted as none of them sounded right for the situation. I eventually decided to write, FOUND HER. SHE IS FINE. GOING TO MEET UP TO TALK WILL KEEP IN TOUCH. The reply was immediate, THANKYOU SO VERY MUCH. PLEASE TELL HER I LOVE HER NO MATTER WHAT PLEASE?

I returned to my room and decided that a drink from the mini bar was a good idea, a small gin might help me convince myself of my own justified deceit. One gin on top of three which I had with my meal, was enough to send me to sleep for the next three hours, which went against my plan of a short power nap.

I woke that evening to the sound of a band playing out on the terrace to entertain the evening diners. The sun had just begun to set and the view from my balcony was close to what I was sure that heaven would look like. The sky was full of bright pinks and reds and the sea was so still it resembled glass. I sat on the balcony and for a few precious moments, I forgot all of my worries as I lost myself in the sunset.

I decided to dress for the evening and go eat out, which I thought was a brave move for a woman on holiday alone. I had no doubt in my mind where I would go and feel comfortable on my own, so I took a taxi and headed towards Hammett's place. Unable to describe the restaurant with no name, I requested the driver take me to the nearest street to the restaurant that I knew. The taxi driver seemed like a very charming man and made an effort to make polite conversation with me, putting me at ease. He told me about nice places to eat and gave me a taxi number for my return journey.

"There's a quaint little place just right of this square. The chef there is very good. I have heard good reviews - I think it is called 'Moanica's'," the driver said.

"How strange? My name is Monica, thankfully not *Moan*ica. although I have been known to be miserable at times," I laughed as I answered.

The taxi driver dropped me off on the corner of the square and pointed me in the right direction. I knew where I was and wandered towards Hammett's restaurant like an old friend returning from their travels. As I walked towards the restaurant I could hardly believe that a sign had been erected in the front of the restaurant. Hand-painted on old wood, it hung above the door proudly displaying the name 'Moanica.' I dare not believe that he had named the restaurant after me, but the hope that it may be true, made me feel like screaming out loud with excitement. I quickly took a picture of the sign on my phone as evidence, feeling this may not be too good to be true.

I excitedly went inside and was shown to a table by a young waitress who had not seen there before. I felt a sense of belonging in this place and almost felt like the waitress should identify herself to me, as if she where the visitor. She politely took my order and handed it over the bar, where it was picked up and taken to the kitchen.

I sat for a few moments, starting to wonder what the hell I was doing going there to eat alone, when the young lady returned with bread asking how I would like my steak?

"Tell chef I like it well done and this time I am not here with a food critic." I found myself falsely laughing hysterically, as if I had said something hilarious. I hated myself that I had lowered myself to act so pathetically just to get the attention of a man. The waitress just stared at me and smiled courteously as she obviously had no idea what I was talking about. I tried to make amends saying, "Sorry - private joke" but I just sounded more stupid as I continued to laugh awkwardly.

As she glided away, I took a large slug of my gin to compensate for the fact that the floor had not opened up to swallow me. The waitress walked to the kitchen and with the return swing of the doors, Hammett ran from the kitchen, picked me up off my feet and swung me around. He was elated. It was as if we were long lost lovers. He kissed my cheek over and over as he shouted to everyone (who cared to listen) that I was his 'Moanica' and after whom he had named his restaurant.

Embarrassingly, I tried to correct him, explaining that my name was actually 'Monica' but as he swept me of my feet, my hair ended up falling into my mouth, and I ruined the whole Officer and a Gentleman thing as I spluttered out the words. I made sure my dress was not pulled up exposing my Bridget Jones knickers as he lifted me from the floor. A party of six on the table behind clapped at his announcement; although I was pretty sure they had no idea what he was talking about.

He took my hand and led me to the front of the restaurant to show me the sign. I tried in vain once again, to explain that my name was misspelled, but he did not seem to understand. I decided to not spoil the moment and to simply enjoy it. I was overwhelmed by his gesture and a misspelling was not going to spoil that.

That evening we ate and drank and talked for hours. Hammett would run off to the kitchen when he was needed but returned quickly to be with me. Conversation between us was effortless, despite his brave attempts at broken English and my futile attempts to speak the three words of Turkish I knew.

Energy and excitement shone from him as he chatted to me, and the evening went by quickly, as all the other diners came and went. I was given priority treatment with attention, drinks and food, I felt like a queen. When the restaurant was closing, Hammett walked me back to my hotel. The walk took over forty minutes, but felt more like five as we walked, talked and laughed. He held my hand all of the way like a true gentleman. When we arrived at the hotel, he stopped at the gates, making no attempt to come in. He kissed my hand and said, "Tomorrow I pick you up. I show you the most beautiful beach in the world." I watched as he walked away, turning back to blow me a kiss.

The next morning could not come soon enough. I hardly slept with the excitement I felt - like a teenager going on a date. I looked at the picture of the restaurant sign on my phone over and over again; I still could not believe it.

The next morning, I was up early and dressed for the beach. I waited in the foyer, unsure what time he would arrive. The concierge waved for my attention, to say there was a car waiting for me. Parked out front was an old beetle car and Hammett sat at the driver seat wearing shades and beaming with excitement. I climbed into the car feeling like a leading actress in a movie as we drove off. A picnic basket lay on the back seat of the car with a large red blanket.

We drove for over twenty minutes and headed for Blue Rock Cove. I climbed down the steep stairs onto the beach and I was overwhelmed at the beauty of the clear sea, blue sky and overhanging rocks. Hammett handed money over to a gentleman at a small car park at the base of the steps. As we walked to the sand I saw the gentleman place a barrier over the steps preventing anyone else from entering the beach.

"Oh, my goodness! Do we have this full cove to ourselves?" I asked.

"Well, yes, but sadly only for the next two hours," Hammett answered.

It was like a scene from a movie as we sat and ate fine food and drank wine. We swam in the sea, then chatted as we lay in the sand under the blazing sun. Hammett told me so much about himself and his family. He explained that he had never married, as he had never met the right person. He talked about Belinda and said it was sad that women like her were often conned, and it was a sad sign of the times as younger men wanted to be 'kept' in life.
Conversation between us was effortless and he made me feel so comfortable in a way that no-one ever had done before. As we left the beach, he helped pack up the picnic things and carried the heavy bag. He held my hand as we left the cove, making me feel like the only woman in the world.

That evening, we ate at a tavern a few miles along from the cave. It was a small, old building that only seated ten people. Hammett said it was the best-kept secret in Turkey as the food was divine. It lived up to its expectation, as we sat in a window seat with the shutters open, eating good food as we watched the sun set. I felt so comfortable and at home as everyone who passed seemed to know Hammett and greeted him with pleasure. His friendly persona shone, as he seemed to know everyone personally, and had some act of affection for everyone he spoke to, asking how family members were or how business was.

We stayed together at my hotel that night, and I felt like time had stopped in some way, and that life could not get any better. I was awe-struck during my time with him, I completely forgot about my life and my past. Life's burdens seemed to lift from my shoulders. He seemed so happy to be with me - he made all of my inhibitions disappear. My body-conscious-self seemed to fade away and was replaced with a confident, happier version of myself. We lay in bed the next morning, naked and wrapped in sheets as we ordered room service and drank coffee as we talked about anything and everything.

That morning, he asked me if I had any plans, and completely forgetting why I had gone there in the first place, I quickly answered 'no' in anticipation of what he had in mind.

We dressed and left the hotel heading for the local market. The day had an exciting buzz about it as we shopped for fresh fruit and vegetables for the restaurant. The market was vibrant and packed with local people all going about their daily business. They all chatted as they passed and were so friendly. We tasted samples of cheeses from one stall and stopped for coffee, eating fresh bread and cakes as we sat. I saw fruits that I did not recognize and vegetables I would not know what to do with. We walked and talked as we shopped and I was amazed at the bartering between them to decide a price.

We headed back of to the restaurant, where I spent the full day chatting to customers and helping behind the bar. The days seemed to fly by; I felt part of the staff. People were happy to be there and had interesting stories to tell. Some people had returned year after year and others were there for the first time. Never in my life had I saw myself as a hostess, but I felt as if I has found my niche in life.

I returned to the restaurant every day that week and spent the late evenings with Hammett at my hotel. I found myself eager for life for the first time in such a long time. I invited Belinda and Temarh over to Hammett's to eat, as I had not seen her since the wedding. I actually looked forward to seeing her and had the staff set a table decorated with candles and white flowers. Hammett made them a special small wedding cake and had their place settings made from red card hearts.

I stood in the kitchen, tasting the new chili and tomato soup that Hammett was experimenting with, ready for the release of the new menu. The bar maid came into the kitchen to tell me my friend had arrived. I was so excited to see Belinda and rushed out to greet her. The feeling was not mutual and she stood alone and actually looked angry with me.

"This is a turn up for the books then - what are you now? The hostess with the mostest?"

I was lost for words and could not think of an appropriate reply. "Let's take a seat; I have put us on this table. Where is Temarh?" I asked, noting his obvious lack of presence.

Belinda almost seemed as she had practiced her reply a number of times over. She confidently explained that he had been called away for a family emergency, so they had only had one night together. She told a tale of how his mother had cancer and had taken a sudden turn for the worst.

I expressed my sympathies and explained that I had not known his mother was even ill. Belinda was vicious in her reply, reminding me that there was no reason that I would know, as Temarh was such a private man and that he had told no-one as he wanted to make sure their wedding day was not spoiled. She went on to say how selfless he was, as he was willing to sacrifice his time with her to be at his mothers' side, at a time when she needed him.

The conversation after that became uncomfortable. All topics of conversation seemed taboo. I asked if she was going to visit his family, to which she replied, "No, it's is not the done thing in Turkey and Temarh is so proud I did not want to push things. It is enough that he knows I am here when he needs me."

I popped into the kitchen to ask Hammett if there was anything that we could do, but he shook his head and said it was best that I did not interfere. I asked if what she was saying was even true, and Hammett simply shrugged his shoulders as if to say 'who knows.'

Belinda spent most of the evening quizzing me about Hammett and what my plans were. She made no attempt to seem happy for me, almost giving the impression she was angry with me.

When I explained that none of what had happened was intentional, but that life had never felt so good, she replied with, "How sad - you fly home tomorrow then?"

The tone of the evening was set at that point and we hardly spoke again as we finished eating and she left in a taxi. Hammett finished up in the kitchen and joined me with a coffee on a table outside. He said not to be so hard on her, as things were complicated for her. He said that she was in love and would only see the things she wanted to see. Friends are there to support you when life is shit, and to be happy for you when things are good.
"Well, why isn't she happy for me now, then?" I asked.

He smiled as he asked, "Are things really good for you?"

"Things feel better than they have been in such a long time." I told him how life had never seemed so care free, and that the thought of going home made me feel so sad.
"You don't have to you could always stay here with me? I think we make a good team."

I could hear the voice in my head screaming out to say 'yes yes yes' but found my mouth giving reasons to justify why I had to go home. I talked about my parents and Rue and Hammett reminded me about the obvious responsibilities of my very successful career (which I had just ever so slightly over exaggerated).

"Yes, obviously I have to work," I replied, as if to try to enforce the truth that hid my lies. We spend that last night together and Hammett left very early that morning to go to market. Hammett said that he would leave quickly, as goodbyes were not his thing and he would ring me before I boarded my flight. He seemed distant and colder than he had all week. I felt so heavy-hearted as I packed my things. I checked my mobile phone a number of times but nothing. I took my case to the lobby and asked for a cab to the airport.

"There is transport already arranged and paid for, Miss," the concierge said.

"Paid for by whom?" I asked.

"I am not sure, Miss. I was just informed that there is a car waiting and it is paid for and to inform you when you rang for a cab."

A chauffer waited to take my bag and I was driven to the airport in a beautiful silver Mercedes. When I arrived at the airport, the driver handed me an envelope and carried my bag to a trolley. I had only taken one bag which weighed very little, so I thanked him and smiled politely until he drove away, then took my case in my hand. I sat in the airport with my luggage at my side and began to read the letter.

I had expected a longwinded letter from Hammett declaring undying love, but it was not as I thought. It simply read, 'Stay.'

I sat for a moment with the note in my hand, wondering if leaving was actually my only option. A feeling of excitement suddenly rose inside me of the fact that I actually had a choice. I questioned myself about what the right thing was to do. Should I go home and beg for my job back that which was practically stolen from me, or should I sit alone and wait for the odd text from a daughter who was busy living her own life? Rue was happy at Mum's and she gave Dad a reason to get out of the house every morning. On the other hand, I hardly knew Hammett and here I was thinking of leaving my life for him, without really knowing him. I tried to assure myself that if I stayed it did not have to be forever. It was just for now - like an extended holiday? My mind was made up. I was arguing with logic and common sense - neither of which felt attractive. I picked up my bag and left the airport.

My perceived image of me running into his arms completely played out as I left the taxi and ran to the restaurant. Hammett was stood out the back smoking, as I ran to him. Just as in my best daydreams, he picked me up and swung me around crushing me tightly in his embrace. I giggled like a schoolgirl as he stood me on the floor.

"Are you staying?"

"I am. I couldn't leave. I have no plans, but yes - I am staying!" I beamed as I answered. He hugged me again.

"I didn't even know you smoked. We don't know so much about each other - it has been such a whirlwind," I said as we stood holding hands.

"I don't normally smoke - you drove me to it, this is what you do to me," he answered then kissed me.

I completely lied in my phone calls home, making the excuse of an extended holiday to everyone. I gushed that I had made new friends and wanted to stay for a while. I explained to my mum that I had been given an extended break from work for working so hard on the Briggs and Lace contract.

"Well, you enjoy it, my love. You worked hard on that and it is like a bonus. Don't worry about Rue - he is fine and your dad is enjoying having him, if the truth is known. Keep in touch though, because you know that I worry. Please don't forget that your Dad has got his appointment with the heart specialist in two weeks? I'm sure it's nothing, but he frets."

I hated myself for lying to my Mum but justified it as an exaggeration of the truth in a way of protecting her. My mind wandered off into thoughts of being happy and settled there in the sun and bringing them over to enjoy retirement. My daughter was not as easily fooled and begged me to be careful and not make any rash decisions. She even had her father book me an open return flight home in case I needed it.

"I am not being captured by a sex slave gang. I'm having the time of my life," I explained, trying to reassure her.

"No, Mum, you're having a holiday, so remember that when you make decisions it's just that holiday feeling, not real life. The sun makes things look better mum."

Staying there for a while longer meant I could no longer stay in a five-star hotel, so accommodation was now a small flat above the restaurant. I took my bags to the room and sized up the place I was to call home for a while. The bland room and tiled floor made it look 'grotty' and its level of cleanliness did nothing to improve that. Dirty old curtains hung from the windows and Hammett's clothes lay scattered across the floor. With no concept of negativity in mind, I set to work cleaning the place, scrubbing floors and cleaning bathrooms.

That afternoon, I walked along to the market, taking the dirty curtains and washing to somewhere they could be cleaned. People welcomed me like an old friend. I had coffee and talked to an ex-pat who had moved there ten years ago to open an Internet business importing chestnuts. At the launderette, I chatted to the women and one of them gave me a flowered scarf that was left over in the washing as I packed up my things. I rolled the scarf and tied it around my head as a headband. I glimpsed at my reflection in the window and was pleasantly surprised at the woman staring back at me. I was previously the type of woman who would go to the hairdresser and asked for the same style of haircut, then smile politely as she showed me the finished style in the mirror even though I still never liked it. Today was different; I actually liked the woman I saw.

I bought flowers on my way back to the restaurant and rehung the curtains. Excited to show Hammett the room, I went to the restaurant to ask him to come and look, but the staff said he had gone out. Not to be deterred, I made myself busy and ironed and hung all of Hammett's clean clothes alongside my own, arranging our shoes in the wardrobe as 'his' and 'hers', psychologically cementing my sense of us as a couple.

He had returned within the hour, but when I asked where he had been he avoided the answer and commented on my scarf saying it made my blue eyes stand out. I showed him the room, which he seemed to love and said he had never felt so looked after, as he had always taken care of himself and home making was a male thing. I felt useful and appreciated as I walked around the tiny flat, pointing out each and every little thing that I had done and he smiled in response.

As we lay in that bed that night, I felt that being with him in there made me feel like I was in a five-star hotel. He commented that he loved the flowers that I had chosen and said they would be beautiful in the restaurant. He said that the business needed a woman's touch and that he had noticed how great I was with the customers.

The next few weeks seemed to pass in a haze of sunshine and fun. I worked every day in the restaurant, learning new skills and a new language. I watched from the bar as Hammett flirted with the customers, dancing as he served them their food. I smiled proudly, knowing that this man loved me and I was his woman. Customers loved his jovial manner and his dance moves. Women, both young and old, would get up from their seats, charmed by his request to dance with the beautiful ladies. He would snap the ends from flowers and place them in the ladies' hairs, often making them gush and always making them want to come back to the restaurant to eat again. Every day, I bought new scarves and wore them in my hair. I felt I had become a new woman - a better version of myself.

After a few weeks, we took a car journey to meet his family. I had imagined his family home to be far away in the countryside, but it was actually twenty minutes away in the centre of a built-up, rather ramshackle, town. His family home was a third floor flat in what looked like a war-ravaged concrete jungle. To get to his family, we had to pass a number of flights of stone steps and some flats, all of which seemed to be over spilling with families of young children. Washing hung along the stairwells alongside sweeping brushes and mops. We had only ever talked briefly about his family, and I wasn't sure how many brothers and sisters he had. I knew that his father was a large part of his life, but I realized that I did not actually know any of their names. I followed behind him along the narrow corridors until we stopped on the fourth floor. The corridor was really hot as the sun blazed through the gaps in the decorative stonewalls and I could feel myself starting to perspire.

A small boy of five or six ran to Hammett, jumping into his arms to hug him. Hammett spoke to the boy, kissing his cheek, and then putting him down as the boy quickly ran off into the flat shouting something excitedly. The front door was ajar. I followed Hammett into the flat.

His mother sat in an armchair on the far side of the room, expressionless at our entrance. The room was sparsely decorated with blandly with cream walls and minimal furniture. A picture of a young soldier took pride of place on a small wooden table which was covered with a dated embroidered cloth. Hammett spoke to his mother, and as if he had just given her permission, she then smiled and stood to greet him kissing his hand. Three more small children came into the room running around chasing each other. Their enthusiasm seemed to aggravate Hammett and he snapped at them to which they responded by quickly leaving the room.

His mother seemed to ask him questions about me as he held my arm, pushing me forward to meet her. She nodded and shook my hand in an uncomfortable manner, as if neither of us knew how to greet one another. She made me feel uncomfortable as she rather rudely pulled my scarf from my shoulders to cover my head. Feeling like I had done something wrong, I left the scarf around my head and pinned it with a hairclip to keep it in place. I felt that in some way I had disrespected her and I felt uncomfortable.

Hammett beckoned me to sit, but with only two chairs in the room, I uncomfortably sat on the floor. A young girl brought us some tea in small glass cups and she giggled as she handed one to me. Hammett and his mother chatted away as I sat politely sipping at my tea.

The first sip made me feel sick. I tried to hide my dislike of the tea, but I was not quick enough to avoid his mother's purse-lipped disapproval. With her lips tensed as though sucking lemons, she raised her voice as she spoke to Hammett, pointing at me as she spoke. The tea tasted of menthol and the thought of trying to finish it to not be rude, made me feel nauseous. I managed to finish my cup, and much to my horror, a further cup was brought. Feeling that enough was enough; I smiled politely but made no attempt to drink the second cup.

We stayed for over an hour as they chatted. I could not be involved in any of the conversation, and at times it seemed heated and not particularly friendly. There was no mention of his father and no signs of a male presence in the home. The flat seemed transient, insomuch that apart from the photograph, nothing seemed personal to the family. The floor was carpeted with rugs that lay on top of one another in a hap-hazarded manner.

I had imagined his family home to have a kitchen at the heart of the home, where family interacted and food was cooked throughout the day, as if in abundance. The kitchen in the flat could be seen through the door and it was a simple kitchen with two cupboards and a sink and again, all very sparse. I was relieved when Hammett said we were leaving, and from my position on the floor, with great difficulty I stood to my feet. My hip and knees ached from sitting in that manner, and my joints cracked as I stood up. His mother laughed and pointed at me and said something. It was the first time I had seen her smile. So glad I could amuse... She held out her hand and Hammett took my purse from my bag, taking out seventy pounds and handed it to her. I had no time to argue I just wanted to get out of there. He apologized, saying it was tradition to leave money and that he had forgotten his wallet, asking if I minded. I felt like saying it was too late if I had minded as the money was gone, but I simply smiled and nodded as if in some strange way it was okay.

Hammett seemed angry in the car as we drove home and snapped at me when I tried to make conversation. When we got back to the restaurant, I went straight to the room and lay on the bed as he headed for the kitchen. I was angry with myself for having such unrealistic expectations of how life would be here, as if my life was part of a film.

After an hour or so, Hammett came to our room and apologized for snapping at me, explaining that taking a woman to meet his mother was a big deal and he had handled it badly. He spoke of Turkish culture and how his family had old-fashioned ways which made things difficult at times. We never visited his family again or spoke about why his father had not been there.

For the next few weeks, life continued to be bliss. I swam every morning in the local hotel pool and lost over a stone in weight. I felt fit and ate healthily, eating fresh fruit every day and walking for miles. Customers would bring me scarves for my hair that they had bought from local markets, as if this was my new signature look.

We would picnic in the evenings, with Hammett cooking new foods for me to try. Twice a week he would play football with his friends, and I would go along to watch. He was good at playing the fool and making people laugh - he was very much the centre of attention when he was with his friends. They treated me very well. I was always made to feel welcome by his friends and their wives; I had never felt so much like I belonged.

After football we would go to barbeques at his friend's home, with Hammett always becoming the chef. The days flew by and I was the most contented I had ever been in my whole life. At times, when I rang home, I had so much to talk about that I often forgot to ask how other people were. My life back home had faded away far into the distance.

Chapter 7

I had been in Turkey for nine blissful weeks. As I sat having a coffee at the restaurant, a young man walked by with a puppy on a lead. I felt my heartstrings pull as the pup stopped at my feet, wagging its tail for a fuss. The pup looked so much like Rue when he was younger. My heart ached as I realized how much I missed him.

With my thoughts now directed on home, I rang my mother. She took such a long time to answer that I started to have a bad feeling that something might be wrong. I was about to hang up when I heard her voice. She answered as she always did, reciting her phone number to ensure you had called the correct one.

"It's me, Mum," I answered, feeling relieved to hear her voice.

"Oh. Can I ring you back? your father is having one of his episodes with his heart and I am giving him his spray in the garden?" With no further explanation, she hung up leaving me in limbo and sick with worry.

That evening, Hammett left work early to do some business that I did not enquire as to the nature of, as my interference was obviously not welcomed. He was gone for over five hours and returned drunk and in a nasty mood. I had never seen him that drunk before and was taken aback by his attitude towards me. I tried to explain about my conversation with my Mum, and that I should return home, but he childishly put his fingers in his hears and sang, "bla bla bla."

Furious at his behaviour, I grabbed my coat and told him I was leaving. As I stood in the doorway, he moved across the bed and kicked the door. The door slammed into the side of my head cutting my ear.

I cried as I ran down the stairs, with very little idea of where I was going to go. I sat outside of the closed restaurant, nursing my bleeding ear with serviettes that had been left on the table. For the first time since my arrival there, I realized how completely alone I was. For the next two hours I cried with a mixture of self-pity and shock. The night grew colder and I eventually headed back to the flat. Hammett lay sleeping in his drunken stupor. I lay next to him, making all efforts not to bodily touch him and I eventually fell asleep.

I awoke next morning to find a flower on the pillow where he had been laid and a note explaining how very sorry he was. He had been alone so long, he was struggling a little to adjust. The note begged me to stay, and with written word, reminded me that I was the love of his life and that he was nothing without me.

Part of me started to accept his apology that it was the demon drink making him not responsible for his actions. But then I read the last line on the note that told me how he hoped my father was okay. If he could not control or remember his action how had he recalled that?

I went down to the restaurant to find life was as normal and Hammett was busy in the kitchen, cooking for a full sitting. I sat at the bar and booked my return flight home for the next day.

That evening, I reflected a lot on my life and what the future could bring. I had not wanted to face the fact that money was now becoming a problem, and that running away from my life was not an answer. I watched Hammett as he worked, feeling now that I had seen another side to him. Strangely though, seeing the nasty side to him in drink made me feel in control, and that by seeing both sides of him, I somehow knew him better and it made me feel confident in myself.

Hammett was on the back foot, making constant apologies and excuses for his behaviour - often kissing my lacerated ear and holding his heart saying that it was a complete accident and he would never dream of hurting a hair on my head.

As we talked that night, I pointed out that I was not some good little Turkish wife who he could treat as he wished. I reminded him that I was there out of choice, and a woman with a home, a life and a career. Even as the words left my mouth I knew that this was no longer the truth, and the need to go home was more urgent than ever.

Hammett cried as he apologized and begged that his failings did not defy our relationship. He talked about how his life would end if I were not his, as it had only just begun when he had met me. He said I was the reason he wanted to live and that before me he felt he had merely 'existed'.

The situation remained strained between us. The following day, I boarded my flight. It was grey and cold outside as the flight landed back home, and there were no welcoming parties for me. As I arrived, I had just a text from Lilley simply saying, 'safe flight.'

It started to rain as I stood in line waiting for a taxi. A couple in front were cuddled together, and they reminisced about their romantic holiday as they sheltered each other from the weather. My heart twinged at the thought of being without Hammett, I felt like half of me was missing.

When I arrived home, the house smelled damp and musky. There was no welcome feel to the house and I did not have the home-coming feeling that I expected to have. I was awoken early the next morning by the sound of the rain tapping against the window; my heart sank at the thought of being away from Hammett.

I left the house early and went out shopping for essentials and called at my mother's afterwards to pick up Rue, knowing that he at least would be pleased to see me. Both my mother and father where sat in the living room, with Rue sat curled up on my fathers' knee. He leapt up to meet me and wagged his tail excitedly. I was shocked that my father looked like a shadow of his former self. My mother saw my look of horror and shook her head as if to warn me not say anything.

"You look very healthy! nice tan," my mother said, deflecting the conversation from my father's illness.

My father did not comment, and Rue went straight back and sat on his lap. I joined Mum in the kitchen where she explained that dad had undergone numerous tests at the hospital, but they were still unsure why he was losing so much weight. She explained that he had developed angina and had so many attacks that this had taken priority to any diagnostic tests. He had been told to try and rest a little to get himself built back up. I felt overwhelming guilt, that while I had been selfish and wallowing in a new life, I had neglected everyone who counted from my old life.

My mother reminded me that it was their forty-seventh wedding anniversary at the end of the week, but due to my father's ill health, she did not want any fuss.

I thought about the sheer enormity of being with someone for such a length of time, and it still not being long enough. For the first time that I could remember, I empathized with her.

I told Mum all about Hammett and my life in Turkey, and she smiled as I explained about my new life.

"I can't wait until you meet him, Mum. You'll love him, I just know you will," I gushed.

"As long as you're sure, dear. You know, relationships take hard work and in day to day mundane situations, they often look different. Your father and I have had our fair share of ups and downs life is not a holiday, sadly."

I returned home and cleaned the house, removing the musky smell. Rue didn't seem all too keen to leave my father and had to be enticed away with treats.

That evening, I stayed up late and chatted to Hammett online. I showed him around my home and introduced him to Rue. He said how much of a handsome dog he was, and that he had always wanted a pet dog but was never allowed one as a child. We chatted about what we would do when he came to England and the places he would like to visit. I talked about my father and he so understood about the full situation, suggesting ways in which we would support my mother if he were to become seriously ill. He asked about work and I skirted around the subject, pretending that when large contracts finished we had a number of months off to recharge.

I looked at the large pile of bills that I had left unopened on the side as I told my lies about work. Hammett chatted about the restaurant and how well the new menu had gone. Talking to him made me miss him so very much.

The next morning, the large pile of unopened letters stacked on the side cabinet seemed to become ever more intrusive and less beckoning, so rather than face them I wrapped them in a band and placed them in a draw out of sight. I promised myself that I would face them the next day.

I spent that morning deciding to be more positive and to look online for a new job. I applied for a number of posts and reluctantly had to name Griff as a referee, hoping he would be kind.

I clicked on 'Visa' and started to look how to apply for Hammett to come to England. The process was extremely complicated and I found it took most of my time for the next few weeks. Application forms and evidence of our relationship were a big part of the process. Financially, it was a bigger deal than I had thought it to be and funds were extremely low. With the thought of a temporary measure, I applied for a payday loan of a thousand pounds, despite my shock at the interest I would have to pay. True to the debt company's word, within minutes the money was in my account and I could click 'apply now' to Hammett's application for a visa. I felt a sense of achievement that that was actually done knowing that it was a means to an end and that we could actually be together and start to enjoy life.

The job application process was a slow one and I spent my days working freelance for an advertising company reviewing documents, and the evenings chatting to Hammett on Skype as he worked. I looked forward to my evenings and would get excited when it was time to call.

I showered that evening and with a glass of wine. I sat in my dressing gown ready to Skype for the evening. I tried to turn on the Internet but it kept saying there was no connection. I tried a number of times, but nothing. After an hour of frustrating attempts, I contacted the network who informed me I had been disconnected due to a number of unpaid bills. In my embarrassment I apologized and blamed a communication error with the bank. The call handler informed me that I had been sent a number of reminders but had not responded. She asked if I would like to resolve the matter and pay my bill to date, to which I made an excuse and declined. I decided to ring Hammett and say there was a problem on the line, but the call just rang and rang and he did not answer. Unable to cope with no communication, I contacted the loan company and increased my loan. I felt sick at the thought of the payments, but even sicker at the thought of not being able to contact Hammett. The loan hardly covered the previous debt I had taken out and left me with only a small amount of money once I had paid for the internet to be reconnected. I added more and more unopened letters to the pile in the draw, continuing to convince myself that once we were together I could concentrate on dealing with them.

It had been five days since we had spoken, despite my attempts at ringing. I was fully aware that he had made no attempt to call me so on the evening the Internet was reconnected I felt sick with nerves at the thought of speaking. I dialled and sat nervously waiting for the connection to be picked up, but nothing. I tried again a number of times, but again with no responses. I began to feel sick at the thought that something may be wrong with Hammett and I had no way of knowing. I started to search for direct numbers to the restaurant and began to frantically dial over and over again, each time receiving a busy tone. After over an hour of dialling, a woman answered the phone.

"Oh, thank goodness! It's Monica. Is Hammett there please? I need to speak to him," I asked with relief that someone had answered.

"Who did you say was calling?" the woman asked. Taken aback that she did not know me, I repeated my name adding that I was Hammett's partner.

Simply answering 'okay' she unintentionally was minimizing my importance for my role in the restaurant. She seemed to take forever. She returned to the phone to apologize but he was unable to speak to me.

"Excuse me? Did you tell him it is Monica speaking?" I answered trying to justify my disbelief of his answer.

"Yes," she replied.

I was dumfounded for a moment until I composed myself and demand she tell him to take my call. She left for a moment, and then returned only to disconnect the call without saying a word. Anger welled up inside me with thoughts of our relationship being false. Ideas that he may have met someone else were only dulled by the idea that he was angry with me for not speaking to him.

I searched for contact numbers on the Internet so I could get a message to him. As I searched, 'Turkish Wives Club' popped up on the screen. I clicked on the page and to my amazement I found a whole forum of women in similar positions to myself. They discussed visa applications, areas where they stayed or lived and openly discussed their relationships. I clicked on key areas of interest and typed in the name of the restaurant. Within a second, a forum of discussion by people that had eaten there and stayed there filled the screen. Comments on how nice the place was and the recommendations of the food were there to read. I clicked on 'gallery' and hundreds of holiday photographs appeared. I scrolled through and found myself smiling at the memories that came flooding back with the pictures of places I recognized.

I scrolled through to find the most recent and found a picture dated a week earlier. I saw an image that made me go cold. There was Hammett, frolicking around at the beach with a young woman and what looked likely to be her son. I scrolled through to see image after image showed them having fun together. They buried each other in the sand and she posed on his shoulders as they went into the sea. They picnicked, just as we had. He had even prepared the foods as he had for me. The picnic blanket was decorated with a small bunch of flowers and the words, 'feeling special' typed along the bottom of the photograph.

Unable to look any further, I drowned my sorrows into a bottle of wine and cried uncontrollably. I questioned how I could get things so wrong. I had planned to grow old with this man. I went to bed that night feeling so heavy hearted, I felt as if I never wanted wake again.

In the early hours of the following morning, I was awoken by the telephone ringing. Half asleep, I jumped from my bed to answer it. My heart lifted as I saw the international number.

"Monica - I am so sorry," I heard him say. His voice was all I needed to hear despite my fears of why he had called. Simply hearing his voice put my world to rights.

I hardly spoke, as he explained that not hearing from me made him think I had left him and he was unable to cope. He talked about how he had not been able to work, losing him so much custom. I asked him about the photographs and he explained that he went to the beach to build up custom as he felt he was to lose the business as well if he did not do something. He explained that the photos were of friendship and nothing more and that no one could or would ever be able to take my place. We spoke for over an hour and it was as if we had not been parted. Hammett said that he felt unworthy of me and that I was so successful and independent that he feared he had nothing to offer me. He talked of waiting his whole life for the right woman, then feeling an overwhelming sense that it had all been too good to be true when I had stopped calling. My heart was lifted as he told me that he had good news for me and that his visa to come to England had been granted.

I felt like my life was back on track and I was in control again. Finances were still a massive issue and the temporary loans I had been getting were no longer an answer. I applied to re-mortgage my house and took on some work, marking test papers for the local college to meet the payments. Assuring myself that this was now a new start, I threw all of the bills that I had been ignoring into the fire and decided that from now on anything sent to me would be dealt with.

I booked a flight for Hammett and decided to surprise him with a business class flight. I paid for a decorator to repaint the house and bought new soft furnishings and a larger double bed to replace my queen size bed. I bought a large television system for the living room with an impressively large screen and surround sound. Everything was falling back into place. My father started to pick up and had gained weight and the freelance advertising company I had been working for were so impressed with my work they asked if I would like to be considered for a permanent position.

The days waiting for his flight seemed to pass so slowly, we talked throughout the day and night endlessly. My heart practically sang as we made plans for the future, we talked of living the summers in England and the winters in Turkey. Hammett spoke of a career as a chef and maybe opening a small restaurant. We planned to see places in England that he had always wanted to see such as Big Ben and London Bridge. I told him of places there where we could eat that he would love. The future was exciting!

The morning he arrived, I was up early and the house was sparkling clean and smelling of new paint. I had my hair and nails done and had found a little black sexy dress to wear for the occasion. I had not told him about the business class ticket as I had wanted to keep it a surprise and was excited to hear what he thought. I waited at Arrivals with over an hour to spare and counted away the minutes in coffee shops as I watched the screens for the announcement of his flight. My heart lifted as I saw him come through the sliding doors and I ran to greet him. His smile was broad when he saw me and he dropped his case and threw his arms around me. We chatted the full journey home about our plans, in my excitement I almost forgot to ask him about his flight.

"It was okay," he said when I raised the question.

"Just okay?" I was shocked at his reply. Then he carried on chatting and I realized it was actually the first time he had flown and thought all flights were the same, so was not as impressed as he may have been as he had no comparison. I giggled at my failed attempt to impress and did not say anything further about the issue.

I had scented candles burning with the log burner lit to welcome him to his new home as we arrived. He smiled when he saw the house. Rue ran to greet us both but Hammett merely patted him to get down as he was tired from travelling and wanted to settle.

I ordered food for us that evening, and we sat in front of the fire talking and laughing as we ate. Having him share my bed that evening made me feel like life was complete. It was as if we had never been apart, as we made plans for life and spent the next two weeks travelling across the country, first class on trains.

We visited London and photographed all the places he had only once dreamt of seeing. I posted pictures on Facebook of my new perfect life. We travelled to the Lake District where we hired a boat to sail for the day, staying in a luxurious boathouse for the night, spending the evening drinking wine on our own jetty as we watched the sun set behind the rolling hills.

Hammett cooked beautiful meals of an evening and we would walk Rue along the beach afterwards. Walking along the beach, Hammett ran ahead and wrote 'marry me' in the sand. My life had never felt so complete. I took a picture of his proposal and popped it in a frame to become a forever memory of a wonderful time.

I loved his spontaneity, he would hand pick flowers and make little arrangements in jars around the house. He would cook beautiful meals and bake cakes, there would be messages next to the cake piped in chocolate saying 'I love you too much.' We spent day and night together for the first few weeks and I did very little work and therefore earned very little money.

Hammett brought only a few items of clothing with him. He was a typical man who had just thrown a few things in a bag. My mother commented that my father had been the same, and after their first holiday together when he wore the same clothes all week, she decided that packing his things was her job from there on. It made me happy to chat with my mother about the similarities of our two men, it felt as if in some way it was confirmation that this time I had got it right.

After three weeks together, we were to attend a family party. It was the dreaded occasion where I was to put him on display for a barrage of onlookers, each with their own opinion.

We shopped for clothes for him to wear, and I enjoyed seeing him look so good in expensive clothing. When I handed my card over to pay the bill at the clothes shop I felt a lump in my throat.

"That will be £945 pounds please, Madam?" the cashier asked.

I tried to not look so shocked and handed the card over the counter. As she swiped the card, Hammett arrived at the till standing next to me, smiling.
"Is everything okay?" he asked.

"Yes, all fine - just paying the bill," I said as I smiled. As I paid for the clothes, he lifted his arm and placed three shirts and a jumper on the counter requesting the cashier pack those too. The cashier looked at me as if for permission, and I smiled and nodded through my well-hidden grimace.

"Thank you, my love, - you spoil me too much. I will be the smartest man there tonight and you will be proud of me, no?" He said as he held my arm.

That evening, true to his word, he looked handsome and I was so proud to be the woman on his arm. Hammett met everyone in my family and worked his charms on them all. People seemed infatuated by his charms with only the exception of my father who did not comment as such but did not seem overly keen on him. My father would often stay quiet and reserve judgment. I often felt that my mother had enough opinion for them both. Hammett danced around with my Aunt Elaine as she shrieked with delight, holding her sling back kitten heels in her hand.

"Don't you like Hammett, Dad?" I asked.

My father slowly placed his drink on the table and said, "'I'm sure he's a nice man, sweetheart, and as long as you are happy I am."

"That's not what I asked you, though, Dad?" I asked again if he liked him.

"I always think that animals are better judges of character than humans, and Rue doesn't like him. Rue is nervous around him, so I will reserve judgment for now."

I hadn't noted how Rue reacted to Hammett until then really, but as my father said it, I recalled that he never made a fuss of Rue and often said he was in the way. My father had not been himself of late, so I decided to put his remarks down to him being a little over emotional. After all, Hammett had never had a pet and maybe wasn't sure how to act around him.

The family party went on into the early hours, and my head throbbed when I woke the next morning. Hammett was not next to me in the bed which was strange, so I put on my bathrobe and went to find him. I could smell fresh coffee made in the percolator from the kitchen and freshly made croissants stood on the oven under a cloth to keep them fresh.

It was still raining heavily outside, and neither Rue nor Hammett was in sight. I rang Hammett's phone with no answer. I heard a noise at the front door and saw letters drop through the post box. I walked to the door and picked up the letters and opened the door. The wind was bitterly cold and blew straight though the gap. To my horror, I saw Rue tied to the fencepost by a small length of rope, which was so short t he was fastened in an upright sitting position. He shivered with cold and his beautiful red coat was soaked and covered in mud from the patch of earth he had been held in. I ran in my bare feet to untie him, fussing him and apologizing as I tried with great difficulty to undo the knot that held him. He whimpered as I pulled at the rope to try and free him as it caught on his wet fur. I took him into the house and wrapped him in warm towels, still mortified as to who would do such a thing.

Within minutes, Hammett came into the house carrying a number of bags and asking for help to unload more from the taxi that stood waiting outside.

"Where the hell have you been?" I demanded to know. Before he could answer I started to explain what had happened to Rue. He looked at me strangely as if he had no idea what my concerns were and carried on putting bags into the kitchen. I followed him into the kitchen to re-enforce what I had just said.

"It's a dog! It doesn't get cold - it should live outside - you treat it like a stupid baby. You let it on the bed and that's dirty. I cannot live like that, you ask too much of me." He had no remorse that he had tied him up. Annoyingly, my father was correct.

I watched as he unpacked the bags he had bought. Three more bags stood on the floor, one contained a mobile phone and the others a coat and shoes.

"Did you take my bank card?" I asked.

He looked at me with fury in his eyes and replied, "What is this? Why are you talking to me this way?" He threw his hands into the air and stormed into the bedroom. I followed him into the room where he sat on the edge of the bed, smoking a cigarette.
"I do not like smoking in the house - please put that out?"

He took a deep breath through the cigarette and blew the smoke into my direction in an act of defiance. "How can you talk to me about not smoking in the house when you let that dirty dog crawl all over you? His hairs are everywhere in the house - it makes me sick. I got up early to cook for you and this is the thanks that I get! You make me feel like I am not the man in this relationship the way you shout orders to me. I am not happy." He stubbed out his cigarette into the empty water glass next to my bed and left the house.

Hammett did not come back for hours and I wandered around the house trying to make sense of the morning. I decided I would take Rue to stay with mother for a while, until things cooled down. Rue seemed more than happy to be going there - happier than he had been for a while. I explained to mum briefly what had happened and she frustratingly answered me sensibly.

"Hammett is Turkish and he has lived there all of his life. You have brought him here, where he has no role in life and no understanding of English ways. We are two different cultures and I am not defending what he did, but you do treat that dog like a baby. Your father is worse. Do you know he made me sit in the back seat of the car last week so the dog could sit in the front? He talks to it more than he talks to me sometimes, and I'm sure the silly dog understands him more than I do these days. He made you breakfast and he is cooking you a meal tonight for you and your friends. I can't get a cup of tea from your father - think yourself lucky. Men are strange, Pet, wherever they are from. You're going to have to be a bit more understanding and give things time."

My mother often had a way of making sense of things that clouded my mind. She was right of course, making her all the more maddening.

Chapter 8

I returned home that afternoon to find Hammett busy cooking. The kitchen was in a state of disarray - he had seemingly used every single pot and pan that I owned to cook. He hugged me as soon as I walked into the room, apologizing for his outburst. He stood behind me held my arms and walked me to the bedroom where he said he had a surprise.

I passed the bathroom to see that the bath had been run for me - bubbles overflowed onto the candles that had been placed around the edges. He held his hands over my eyes as we walked to the bedroom. "You can look now," he said as he moved his hands from my eyes to reveal a dress bag hanging on the back of the bathroom door.

"I bought it for you to wear tonight when your friends come around. I picked it especially, as it so reminded me of you. But first, enjoy the bath and afterwards you can look.

Not feeling as thankful as I maybe should have, I smiled as he kissed me, then returned to his cooking shouting, "No peeping!" as he went.

I quickly looked at the price tag hanging from the bag; eighty pounds all but one penny. My heart sunk as the weight of my finances hung heavy. The bath was only lukewarm and the rose petals he had taken out of the front garden to throw in had become slimy. I could not help to think that I preferred the petals actually on the roses and in the garden.

"Are you relaxing?" he shouted from the kitchen.

"Yes, thank you, it's lovely," I lied. This was something I was becoming good at.

"There's a glass of wine next to your bed all ready for you," he hollered back from the kitchen.

I climbed out of the bath and put on my bathrobe. It was still covered in dirt from the dog earlier, the thought of which continued to make me angry. "Rue is going to stay at my mother's for a while," I replied through pure curiosity, to see what his reply would be.

"Whatever you decide is best, my sweet," he called back.

I put two fingers up in the air and mouthed at him to fuck off. He just missed my pathetic attempts at expressing my feelings as he walked in the room, asking if I liked the dress. I told him I had not looked yet and had only just got out of the shower.

He took one look at my bathrobe and reminded me that it was a good decision to take Rue to my mother's, as things were getting obviously ruined in the house. He took the robe from my shoulders leaving me uncomfortably exposed as I grabbed the towel from the bed to cover myself. He threw the robe into the washing bin and unzipped the dress bag that hung on the door, and with a massive smile across his face asked, "Do you love it?"

If I could tell you everything that I hate in a dress, all of it was there in that monstrosity hanging before me. Bright silver, with a cowl neck and padded shoulders. It was barely long enough to reach my thighs - let alone cover them. It shone like foil in the light, just in case it wasn't eye-catching enough.

"I'm lost for words," I said. Hammett beamed explaining that he knew I would love it and that he thought of me as soon as he saw it. The words 'do you even know me at all' swam through my head but did not leave my lips. He was eager for me to try it on, but I managed to stall him for a while, telling him I had not applied skin cream and would not want to stain it. He left to carry on his preparations for the meal and I sunk onto the bed in a state of despair. I texted Phil to say I was looking forward to seeing him and begged him to not mention the dress.

I held on as long as I could to not have to wear it, but it was nearly seven and everyone were due to arrive. Hair done and make up applied, I dragged the horrible thing over my head and looked in the mirror. I almost laughed out loud at my reflection, as I stood looking at a middle-aged overweight prostitute trying to dress as a teenager staring back at me. Hammett walked into the room his eyes wide with excitement.

"Wow, oh wow wow wow, my sexy woman!" He ran to me, grabbing my backside, telling me how he hoped the night went quickly as he couldn't wait to get me out of the dress.

"I feel the same," I answered, but he did not understand the sarcasm. I felt like crying at the sheer sight of myself as Hammett came into the room to change for dinner. He chatted about the menu he had prepared as he changed into his new clothes. He took his new shoes from the box, passing them to me to ask me to remove the tags.

"You paid two hundred and forty pounds for these?" I asked in amazement as he handed them to me.

"I do not know I paid on the card," he answered. Words failed me as I stood there in my cheap looking dress feeling like I had suddenly woken up in the middle of a bad dream. Hammett changed the subject asking what Phil's wife was called?

"They are not married yet and he is called Warren. He is really nice - you will like him."

"A man and a man together?" he asked scowling.

"Obviously, yes. This is not the dark ages; they will not be stoned in the street, although I think I might be if I go out in this dress," I laughed as I answered leaving the room to answer the door as our guests had arrived.

Hammett had prepared the most perfect four-course meal. He had dressed the table and bought wines that complimented the food. Candles flickered between the flowers on the table casting a warm glow onto the new tea set Hammett had bought with my card. I felt proud to answer the door to Phil, to show him my new life as part of a couple, instead of the wallflower I had been for so many years. As I opened the door to Phil he greeted me with a big smile then stepped back to observe my attire.

"You didn't say the theme was drag? I've come as a man."

"Hammett bought it for me - isn't it lovely?" I said through gritted teeth.

"Beautiful, and I know the very site you can sell that on." Warren laughed as he gave Phil a dig in the arm saying "It's nice that he chose it for you, Monica, and thank you so much for inviting us - I know Phil has missed you," He handed me a bottle of wine and some flowers as Phil sarcastically said, "Just put a straw in the bottle - you deserve it for wearing that."

I formally introduced Hammett to Phil and Warren. Warren went to shake his hand. Hammett apologized for holding a tea-towel, explaining that his hands were covered with flour from the bread and excused himself to go and wash them. We sat at the table as Hammett completed the last finishing touches to the meal and chatted. It was so nice to see Phil and even nicer to see him happy. We talked about old times and some of the things we had done but could hardly finish our stories for laughing.

Hammett was quiet during the meal and I wondered if the language barrier had caused him some difficulties. Warren made several attempts to make conversation with him, asking him how he liked England and about our travels, but Hammett would reply with short answers. The evening seemed to go well and we talked about planning another night at Warren's house so he could return the favour.

"Don't expect food as delicious as this, though. I can work my way around the kitchen but I am no chef," Warren explained.

Hammett left for the kitchen to bring the coffee.

Warren tried once more to make conversation with Hammett. Which part of Turkey are you from Hammett? I know a little about Turkey - my first ever partner was Turkish. He still lives there. He's married now and they have had two children, through surrogacy, I suppose."

The atmosphere in the room suddenly turned to thick fog as Hammett replied, "There are no gay Turkish men." Phil nearly choked on his wine.

"Well there are at least two as they are good friends of ours and they have been together for almost fifteen years," Warren said, as if he needed evidence to defend his case.

In an attempt to lighten the mood, I tried to explain that Hammett was confused and meant gay marriage was not well known among his friends. Hammett swiftly reminded me that he did not require me to apologize for him and he stood by what he had said and got up rudely leaving the table.

Phil and Warren swiftly left with apologies unable to speak to Hammett for anger. I went to the bathroom to remove my make-up and that horrible dress. Hammett sat on the bed and took of his shoes.

I could hardly contain my temper, either, as I removed my eye shadow in the bathroom mirror.

"How the hell could you have such bigoted, old-fashioned views? They are our friends and this is not the eighteen hundreds. I couldn't care less what their sexual preferences are, and frankly, it's none of our business how they choose to live their lives, nor does it change them as friends."

Hammett leapt from the bed and ran to the bathroom pushing my head into the mirror while he spoke through gritted teeth. He held my head fast against the glass as he raged.

"Never again will you disrespect me like that! They will never come to this house again and you will not speak to them." As he took his hand from the back of my head I did not dare to move, and for a few seconds just stood frozen to the spot. I heard the front door slam and he left the house.

I looked at myself in the mirror as black mascara ran down my cheeks carried in tears. I tore off the dress, ripping it in the process, and threw it to the floor. I climbed into the shower and sat on the floor crying for over an hour, before falling into bed alone.

Hammett was already awake and in the kitchen cleaning when I got up. He asked if I would like coffee as if nothing had been done or said the night before. We spoke very little after that. He spent most of the day on the computer or on the phone, so I had no idea what he was talking about or to whom. I finished cleaning the kitchen and the dishes from the disastrous evening before and made two coffees and carried them into the sitting room. I noticed that Hammett had my credit card on the side of the table next to the computer.

"Are you buying something?" I tried to ask as if to sound casual and not furious. His answer was a simple "No.'

"Why is the card there?" I asked the obvious question.

Hammett answered as if I were bothering him by even asking the question.

"Business," he said bluntly, and ushered me away as if I should not be interfering.

I went to my room to check my Internet banking, only to find out that money had been spent without my knowledge. Four separate transactions of two thousand pounds had been sent to an international bank over the past three weeks. With my phone in the air as evidence I stormed into the room demanding to know what was going on. Hammett slammed the computer shut and took the phone from my hand.

"Why are you checking up on me like I am a small boy who is not to be trusted?"

"Well, I wouldn't have to check if you would just be honest and talk to me. We need to talk about money! I haven't got an endless pot of gold," I ranted furiously.

I expected an argument in return and braced myself for the onslaught, but Hammett simply sat with his head in his hands pulling his hair nervously through his fingers. His eyes were red and swollen as he cried and tears fell through his fingers.

"He eventually sat back and took a deep breath. "I have not been honest with you and it makes me ashamed of myself. I want so much for our life to be good, but I was scared that if you knew the truth you would not want me and that I could not bear. I have thought about taking my own life rather than face the shame I feel every morning."

Similar thoughts ran through my head, such as I was thinking I felt the same in that dress but I never spoke. He went on to tell me how he had borrowed money from the restaurant to pay medical bills for his mother. He said he was ashamed to say his father had left his mother and the children to be with another woman and left the family in disgrace. He described how slowly the hospital payments had become unmanageable, but the care she required a necessity.
When I enquired about what was actually wrong with his mother, he said she also had brought shame upon the family, behaving in ways she should not following her husband leaving requiring her to have hospital treatment.

"Did she have mental health issues?" I asked.

Hammett snapped again "No, she was just not well." He was obviously offended by any idea that mental health issues were even real.

"How much have you taken?" I asked.

He held his head in his hands and spoke without facing me, explaining that he initially stole two thousand pounds and tried to repay it by borrowing from a loan shark and the debt had just mounted up out of all control.

"How much do you owe now?" I asked.

His answer made my heart sink, with the thought of no hope as he said he actually had no idea and the people he owed could make this debt endless. He thought that by coming to England he would escape the pressure, but the loan sharks simply turned to his mother causing a greater threat.

We sat for what seemed like hours and we talked and talked. I talked honestly about some of our differences which were making me feel uncomfortable, and he promised to try and understand. After hours talking, we agreed that I would use the last of my re-mortgage money and attempt to pay off the debt once and for all. Although my subconscious was screaming out with warning not to hand over the remnants of my worldly goods, I was in this relationship and his problems had become my problems too. I knew that if it were my mother, I would do anything to help her and admired the same quality in him. When he spoke of the shame of his father leaving, his hurt pride was evident, and the thought that he had inherited a family for whom to care, made me appreciate more why he had never married.

At this point, I so much wanted to be honest about my job (or lack of a decent one) and to admit that I too, had told lies. It was the opportune time to put our relationship onto a clear slate, but I could not bring myself to say the words. My career had been the one thing that helped me through the break-up of my first marriage. It afforded me to keep my pride and my self-respect. Evidently, now I was going to have to work even harder as now the need was greater for us both.

The honesty between us seemed to replace any excitement and passion that we once enjoyed. Days together became mundane and boring. I would spend most days in an internet café marking papers and looking for more freelance work, to try and hold back the financial tide that was about to drown me. The more work I took on, the less I seemed to earn. Work that had previously come easy with the contacts that I had made over the years, was now really difficult. I would return home at the end of the day and make up stories that happened in the office to make my life seem real. I often found myself telling stories of things that had actually happened there in the past. Recalling office events and characters became a therapeutic pastime.

I found myself avoiding invitations to parties which sadly were once one of the things I most looked forward to before meeting Hammett. The thought of making excuses for his stupid dancing at inappropriate times, as if we were still in a Turkish restaurant, made me cringe. The thought of watching him spend more money on clothes as if it were a 'given' made my heart sink. My mother constantly reminded me that relationships were hard work and that there had to be give and take. I had to concentrate on the giving part, as Hammett had given up so much by coming here and leaving his home.

Each day I would leave the house and he would stay in bed asleep. He spent his full day on the computer and most of the very late hours of the night, walking on his own. He stopped shaving and grew an unruly beard that did not suit his face. He stopped changing his clothes and hardly showered. We spent early evenings eating separately - usually sandwiches. Hammett no longer cooked for us both but preferred to cook for himself and freeze meals for later, with stickers on the tubs identifying that they were his. He smoked over forty cigarettes a day which infuriated me, as apart from it being the worst habit known to man, it was also very expensive. He would smoke half a cigarette and throw the stub into the garden, which I would then have to pick up later. Small things that he did seemed to aggravate me the most. I had never noticed before now, but as he ate he made a slight humming sound. The noise was so quiet that at first it was hardly noticeable, but with time it became as deafening as a pneumatic drill.

He would often go shopping for fresh foods for me to prepare for him. He shopped with no expense spared at the most expensive shops, and when I questioned him about it, he would say he did not understand. The late night walks he took became stranger as he would leave the house at midnight and not return until the early hours. When I asked him about where he had been, he just said that that was the most peaceful time to walk. I often thought of following him, but frankly, I could not care enough to get out of bed to meet the challenge. My life felt as if it here on a loop of repeat and there was no way of getting off. I called into see my mother on my way home one day to kill time.

"Your mother is at yoga," my father said in a slightly elated way.

"Since when did she do yoga?" I was intrigued.

"She goes to more classes than a teenager, these days," he answered chucking to himself. "She is chairwoman of the Village in Bloom now, don't you know? There are clipboards all over the house with bits of paper on that mean absolutely nothing at all."

"She never used to leave the house," I said, as if to inform him he must have it wrong in some way.

"Well she never stays in the house now. Not that I am complaining - I enjoy the peace with Rue." Father picked up his paper and put on his glasses. Peering over the top of the rim he asked, "How is that new man of yours managing in chilly England?"

"To be honest with you, things are not going very well at all," I sighed as I answered.

"You know, I'm not one to lecture, sweetheart, but he is like a fish out of water here, and people need a purpose in life. However, that said, life is so short we don't have time to waste being unhappy - that is not fair on anyone."

"The last thing I need is a lecture, Dad. Good advice on what to do would be more useful," I said, hopeful that he had an answer.

Father went quiet for a few moments then said, "I can't tell you about relationships, but I can tell you that a couple of men at the bowling club have said that Hammett is a bit of a strange one and wanders about at night."
I immediately became defensive and explained that it was his culture and he enjoyed long walks to clear his mind. My father was not convinced and pointed out that regardless of what he enjoyed, it was strange and people had noticed. "Sandra Farrow's daughter from Warrell Street rang the police on Tuesday, thinking he was following her home from work. The poor girl has a weak heart you know."

"She is also twenty-stone, Dad, and I don't think he would follow her even if he was a weirdo - which he isn't." I knew too well how people in a small town would gossip at the slightest hint of anything out of the ordinary, and I felt I owed it to Hammett to protect him from their small-mindedness.

That evening, I returned home to find that Hammett had not only cleaned the house but had also cooked a wonderful meal. No explanation was given as to why and I did not ask. Clean shaven, he handed me a new tomato bread he had made to taste with stuffed olives, which he knew were my favourite.

We talked that evening and laughed just like old times. As the days went on, things seemed to get better. We started to make plans for the future. Hammett asked if I could arrange with work for us to travel back to Turkey for the start of the season and maybe to travel around Turkey a little more, as I had only seen such a small part of it. I found myself looking forward to going home from my pretend workplace every day, just to spend time together. It was as if we had come through a bad patch and somehow had managed to survive as a couple.

Weeks went by without any problems and life was good. I continued with my make-believe job, but I did make an active effort to find permanent employment. I had heard nothing from the job for which I had applied, so I decided to chase that up with an email. I planned that if I could get full time employment, I could rebuild my career and put my finances in order. The staff at the Internet café was so used to me working there, that I had my own chair and could order my coffee with just two words 'the usual.' On this particular day, I had worked for over two hours and my eyes began to strain from staring at the computer screen. I decided to go and stretch my legs and wandered across the café to read the notice board. The café often housed the weird and the wonderful of people in society and the notice board was no less colourful. Adverts written on scraps of paper sold everything from old kitchen utensils to sex. A smarter piece of card advertising a room for rent caught my eye.

ROOM FOR RENT
SHARED BATHROOM
NON-SMOKER, NO DRUG USERS.
MUST HAVE REFERENCE
BOND PAYMENT REQUIRED.

The address was familiar I called the number on the card. A female voice answered, "Belinda? Is that you?" I asked.

"Yes, it is! Fancy you calling. To what do I owe the pleasure?" she answered.

"I just wondered how you are? It has been such a long time since we've spoken."

Belinda answered sarcastically, "Well, you're the one who has left it for so long."

I did not want to rise to her comments so asked her if she would like to catch up and have a coffee. She agreed and asked if I wanted to call at her house. "Are you still at the same address? I asked.

"Yes, so if you can remember where it is, feel free to pop around today - if you're not busy."

I did not mention the advert, just agreed to call.

The guilt of neglecting her as a friend was cringe-worthy and I looked forward to seeing her. I bought two cream cakes from the local bakery and called at her house that afternoon. Her once immaculate little garden area at the front of her house was now grey with stones. The window frames were old and the paint flaked from their edges. The curtains that hung from the window were yellow and old. The glass pane rattled as I knocked on the door and I heard a voice shout out, "Come in - the door is open."

I opened the door to a musky smelling passageway with a semi-circle table that had old silk flowers in a vase on it. Belinda looked twice the weight she had the last time I had seen her. Her face looked sullen and she appeared much older. Her hair was cut into a really short style with grey areas at the front. She had dark eyeliner across her eyelids that looked as if it were applied with a shaky hand. Her lips looked thin and the over bright that she had applied in an attempt to make them look fuller, failed. She wore an oversized dress than hung from her hips in an unflattering way, dressed up only by the three brown-beaded necklace that hung around her neck.

Conversation was difficult between us at first, with each of us talking pleasantries. Belinda prepared us both some fruit tea and cake served on a Turkish tea table that she had bought at a flea market. A large photograph of her and Temarh on her wedding day hung on the wall, taking pride of place. She looked so different now to how she did on that day. Belinda saw me looking at the picture and said, "Happiest day of my life, that day."

"How are things with you and Temarh?" I asked the obvious question. Belinda was almost too ready for my question.

"That depends what you are referring to as 'things'?" she answered, leading me to believe that things were not well.

"I don't know if you heard, but I was really ill a few months ago with a blood clot on my lung. I was in hospital for a few weeks with complications. Temarh struggled with me being ill and was, frankly, unable to cope with the heartache."

"So where is he now?" I asked.

"Well, it's a long and complicated story, but the short answer is that he is studying in Edinburgh."

"Studying what?" I asked.

"Engineering - specializing in structural surveying of historical buildings," she said proudly.

"Are you still together as a couple, though?"

"Would you just like me to answer 'no' to that question, so you could join the rest of the world in saying 'I told you so'? Well, I'm sorry to rain on your parade, but yes, we are together. He is right now, in fact, studying to build a better life for us both."

"Are you paying for him to study and live there?" I asked.

"No. We are investing in our lives together, because we are a couple and what we have belongs to both of us."

"Your illness was not for you both then?" I said sarcastically.

Belinda looked furious as if all hell was about to escape from her mouth. "Let's just think about this attitude that you have with me, because glass houses and stones springs to mind. Was it so long ago when you were not the oracle on relationships? You were crying into your wine every night at my house, because your husband wanted a divorce and you couldn't cope. I didn't lecture you - I just supported you through what you described as 'the worst time of your life. Now, I'm not asking for you to return the favour, but I am asking for a little respect. Don't come into my home thinking you have the right to judge me on what I choose to do with my life."

I was taken aback by the energy of her wrath that was followed by tears, which seemed wrong from someone so previously harsh in everything she did. The biggest response I could muster was, "Wine?"

We both started to laugh and Belinda went into the kitchen and poured two large glasses of white wine.

"I shouldn't drink really - I have hardly eaten and it makes me so ill these days I am practically a lightweight," I said as I took a large gollop of wine.

Belinda laughed saying, "Not to worry - I have cake in the fridge that I know goes well with this wine."

We talked for so long, we worked our way through two bottles of white wine, one red and half a lemon loaf cake. We talked about old times and even older relationships. Belinda's husband had remarried and was happily settled with her best friend from her school days. She was called Pamela and had been widowed twice. Belinda laughed about the sheer coincidence that she had Colin insured before the ink was dry on the marriage certificate. She seemed honestly happy that he had settled and talked about how he often popped around with vegetables from his allotment. "We talk more now than we did in all our years of marriage," she joked.

She skirted around the subject of Temarh as I did Hammett. I was no longer in a position to gush about true love. We talked about work and for the first time in what felt like so long, I was able to talk honestly about how my career had taken a nosedive.

"Money must be a problem then?" she asked.

"When is money not a problem to anyone?" I replied.

"I think more cake is in order," she said as she went to the kitchen. "Would you like a vodka?" she shouted.

"I am sure I shouldn't, but what the hell?"
Everything from the first vodka onwards was like therapy. We laughed until we cried as we reminisced.

"What will Hammett think about you being out all day?" Belinda asked.

"I don't give a toss what he thinks - we don't get on as well as I had thought we would. Don't get me wrong - he is not a bad person and we have begun to make things a little better, but it is still difficult. Some days we just don't speak at all. We literally have nothing to say to each other. He goes into such intense moods for no reason and his temper is vicious. Most nights he goes out walking at all hours, and I have no idea why or what he is doing."

Belinda pulled a face with a sideways half smile, "I have heard all about his midnight walks, otherwise known as 'dogging'."

I sat bolt upright from the position I was in from sheer shock.

"What the hell? You must be joking?"

"No not all - he has a bit of a reputation for spending late nights up by Pier Pass and that place is an infamous dogging site. I think it was even on television once on some kind of documentary," Belinda sniggered as she spoke.

I was shell-shocked, unable to process what I had heard. I was equally as upset that I would think him capable.

"Well, what exactly do they do at this 'Pier Point'?" I asked.

"Just watch, I think and obviously I can't say for sure, but that's what they did on the telly."

"Watch what? Other people having sex?" I asked in a genuine state of naivety.

"Yes," she answered as if to enforce my question as being stupid.

"Why?"

"Well, it's not a social pastime with coffee and cakes. Why do you think?" Belinda's answer was scathing.

I settled myself with the fact that there was no evidence to say that was at all the only he went for walks. He often walked late at night back home. Why should being here change that?

"Regardless of what you might think he may or may not be doing, he has gained a reputation around here as a bit of a weirdo. I think we need another vodka," Belinda poured us another.

"People are small-minded in this town, and because he's foreign they think he is weird. That's all that it will be." I think my answer was to assure myself more than her.

We sat quietly for a few moments and I took a deep breath and admitted that I thought he was a little weird, too. I explained to Belinda that I felt as if I was trying to make him into someone he wasn't. I wasn't sure if I had ever loved him at all and was maybe in love with the idea of being in love.

Belinda was very understanding. I expected her to say something sarcastic but she didn't, she simply nodded as if in agreement. She started to talk a little about Temarh and I sat and listened. The image of the foolish old woman was washed from my mind as she spoke honestly about how she knew he did not love her as she loved him, but how he was her last chance at true love, and if it took everything she had to try and make it work, then she was willing to do that. She talked of the extensive efforts that she had gone to prove their love in order to obtain his visa and allow him to study here. She felt that if she made his life good, then part of that life (even if a small one) would be with her.

"I would rather have a small part of something meaningful than a large part of something that meant nothing." In that one sentence she had summed up her whole relationship. In my head I was screaming 'what about you and your self-respect?' but she had obviously already thought of those things, and the intense love she felt for him was no comparison to any loss of self-worth.

Belinda talked about how she had developed blood clots on her lungs following a flight home from Turkey, and how he was supportive but only from a distance with mostly phone calls and texts. Illness was not something she had factored into her mission to find true love. She continued to make excuses for his behaviour - excuses that I am sure even she did not believe. The illness had left her debilitated and unable to work following her recovery. She had taken on advertising work at home to pay the bills and Temarh's educational expenses. The room to rent was Temarh's idea as yet another resource for money to keep him in the life to which he had become accustomed.

Despite how he had treated her, her eyes still glistened as she talked about him. His university timetable took central space under a magnet on the fridge. She took pleasure in knowing which lectures he would be in and would email him with pre-class information in bullet point form, to help him with his studies. It almost seemed like she was talking about her son, and not her husband.

I checked my phone and there were no messages, only a voicemail from my mother, which I decided I would listen to after a coffee. I was in desperate need to sober up. I ordered a taxi as I drank my coffee, and my phone alert went off again, informing me that there was a second message from my mother. Worried that something was wrong, I called the voicemail to listen. I heard my mother's voice awkwardly talking as if I were on the other end of the line, explaining that Hammett was looking for me and that he had called at her house. She asked me to ring back to let her know if I was safe, but not after half nine, as she was having an early night as she had 'one of her heads.' My father said that she had a number of heads but had been highly trained in knowing what to do when she had a headache coming on. I could guarantee that as soon as she announced that she had 'one of her heads' he would have the blinds drawn and eye-mask at the ready and a small concoction of tablets by which she swore.

I really needed to get home…

Chapter 9

The house was in darkness when I staggered through the front door. I could feel a hangover starting already and badly regretted every mouthful of alcohol I had drank. Hammett was nowhere to be seen and the house was cold and untidy, dirty kitchen pots filled the worktops with left-over food and spilled milk that had hardened. The freezer was packed full of prepared meals Hammett had made for himself. I searched through draws for headache tablets finding none, and with no effort to carry on searching, I gave in and headed for the shower.

I felt great relief as the water ran over me as if it was draining the pain from my head. I sat on the floor of the shower covering my head with shampoo and sat on the floor of the cubicle as the shower rinsed my head. As the cubicle steamed up, I began to relax. I almost felt as if I could fall asleep there and then. I heard a faint noise that sounded like the lock of the front door drop. I shouted out to Hammett to let him know I was in the shower. I assumed he had not heard, as he did not reply.

"Hammett? Is that you?" I shouted again as I wiped steam from the glass door. I rinsed the soap from my eyes and could see Hammett's body shape as he opened the shower door. Without saying a single word, he grabbed me by my hair and dragged me across the cubicle floor and out of the shower. I screamed as I tried to hold my hair close to my head to stop him from pulling on it. The pain was incredible. I screamed at him to stop, but he took no notice as he dragged me into the bedroom. He lifted me to my feet by pulling harder at my hair, as he then threw me naked onto the floor. I screamed and cried and begged him to stop, but as he let go of my hair he punched me in the face. Blood burst from my nose as he quickly grabbed at my hair again, as if to secure his hold on me and punched me again. I felt as if my cheek would explode as he twisted my hair to grab it harder then used my hair to lift me to my feet and drag me into the front room.

His eyes where scarily wild and angry - he seemed to look straight through me. He spoke in Turkish spitting as he spoke with such venom. He picked up a letter from the table and told me to open it. With shaking blood-covered hands, I trembled as I opened the letter. It was an invitation for Phil and Warren's wedding. He grabbed the invitation from my hand, then screamed in my face as he tore it up, throwing the scraps of paper at me as I sat crying.

"You will never disrespect me again. This is what you make me do. I told you to have nothing to do with these people." He said as he left the house, not looking back as he slammed the doors behind him.

He was gone for hours. I wandered the house trying to compose myself. My head felt like it would explode as I now more desperately hunted the house for painkillers. I cleaned up the blood from my nose that had leaked onto the bedding and the floor, leaving pink stains in the cream carpet as I rubbed. I put frozen peas on my face to reduce the swelling but could not control my tears. I lay in bed looking at photographs on my phone - memories of holidays I had spent with Phil and Grace. Tears flowed from my eyes as happy memory after happy memory replayed in my mind. How the hell had I ended up in this predicament? My pillow was damp and bloodstained and only the alcohol dulled the thudding, unbearable pain in my head.

I awoke when Hammett arrived back home in the early hours of the morning, slamming the front door as he entered. I pretended to be asleep as he got into bed and waited until he was asleep. I crept out of the bedroom so as not to wake him. I showered and dressed as quietly as I could and attempted to apply make-up over the reddened areas on my face. I looked at my reflection, feeling as if I should be black and blue but had only small red marks on my face. I had scratches and small bruised areas to my legs where I had been dragged from the cubicle. My war wounds did not do justice to my experience. I somehow wanted a large blackened eye that I would present as concrete physical evidence of my ordeal.

I dressed in loungewear that morning, as comfort seemed the order of the day. I was unsure where to start to gather my thoughts, so I decided to clean the house, as if to clear my mind. It was very cold outside that day, so later that morning I put on my large coat and went into the garden to prune the plants as the season was now at an end. Children ran around in the grove, excited for Halloween. Next door had decorated their full garden with pumpkins and cobwebs and with a sign on their front door saying, 'Enter if you dare!' I decided to go out and buy some sweets for the trick or treaters to take my mind off my issues.

I returned around two hours later with a pumpkin I had bought to carve and a bowl shaped like a spider's web in which to put sweets for the children. My stomach churned with anxiety as I turned the key unsure of what to expect. I placed my shopping in the hallway and went into the living room. Hammett was in the kitchen smoking a cigarette and exhaling out through the open kitchen window. At a glance I could see that the pots and pans that I had cleared earlier had visibly piled up again.

"I'm home" I said, knowing fine well he knew that I was but had chosen not to speak.

I took off my coat and placed it onto the back of the sofa. In the living room the occasional table had been moved from its usual place at the side of the sofa and placed in the middle of the floor. It was covered with an old-fashioned flowered pillowcase used as a tablecloth. A large photo frame stood central to the small table. I turned it around to see a faded photograph of Hammett's friend who had been killed in the army. The photo was faded but areas had been touched up with bright colour making it look eerie. For a few seconds I wondered if it was an attempt at Halloween decoration, until I noticed that he had nailed five large plastic roses to the front wall with oversized nails. Images of his mother's drab flat swam through my head making me feel sick with anxiety.

Hammett walked in from the kitchen, still blowing smoke from his lips as if to aggravate me. He seemed nervous and twitchy as he stared at me but did not speak. He took the photo frame from my hand and placed it back onto the table as if to return some precious jewel to its rightful place. He then sat on the sofa and put his head into his hands.

I attempted to broach the subject of what had happened. "Last night ……."

Before I could finish my sentence, Hammett jumped to his feet as if he had just exploded and started to rant. He shouted about how he was ashamed of me and that he felt unable to carry on loving me if I planned to continue to behave in this way. He raised his sleeves to expose large scratches on his arms that he said I had done, as he attempted to place me safely into bed. He spoke of my violence as a drunk and how he had had to get me out of the shower for my own safety. I had flayed my arms around to hit him and he had been concerned that I would smash the glass shower screen and hurt myself. My head spun with self-doubt. Had I really got it so wrong? I touched my cheek then winced with the pain, in an attempt to prove that my memories were real and not from some drunken imagination. He saw me wince and told me that he was pleased that I hurt, and to let it be a reminder that my actions had consequences. He stood to his feet, waving his arms in an attempt to re-enact how I had thrown myself onto the floor and hit my face on the bed frame. He carried on his verbal onslaught until I found myself apologizing to him for my unacceptable behaviour.

The mood that evening was a sombre one, despite his efforts to cook a meal for us both. My conversation seemed to be overburdened by the words 'thank you and sorry' as if I was an obedient wife. He poured wine with our meal that I dare not decline, but just sipped as the thought of drinking any alcohol turned my stomach.

"I saw you doing the garden today," he said in an attempt to make polite conversation.

"I was just removing a few weeds and pruning," I answered as I looked at my grubby hands. I noticed that my nails were still short as I had not had a manicure for some months. I looked at the scratches on his arms and with a sick feeling in my stomach realized I had not at been responsible for the scratches. I suddenly felt scared of him and looked across the table at a man I did not know. The thought that he had scratched himself to support his lies was a thought with which my mind could not cope.

"Why is there no money in the bank?" he suddenly asked, dragging me from my thoughts.

I stuttered as I said, "Isn't there any in there? My wage should have gone in yesterday - I will have to check," I said to provide support to my lies. There was no money. I had not earned enough. The bills were not paid and I felt as if I was drowning in debt. I had applied for a debt consolidation loan of which I was in the process of arranging - it was to be my lifeline.

"I need to send money home and there is nothing there. I think you should go to the bank and sort it out," he said, as if it where that easy.

"I didn't realize that you were sending money home. How much were you planning on sending?" I asked as if it were just out of interest and not a desperate question on which my financial situation hung.

"Do you see a small boy sat here?" he asked.

"What do you mean?" I asked, genuinely perplexed by his question.

"I asked you if you see a small boy that you think you are allowed to question about money? Or do you see a grown man? Tell me, Monica, what do you see?"

"I see a grown man, obviously. I was merely enquiring as to how much you needed?"

He swiftly got up from his chair and took the plates from the table to the kitchen as if he was unable to tolerate my presence. He took the dishes to the sink and smashed them into the basin one after another. Then, as always at that time of evening, he took his coat and left the house without explanation.

As if this had now become the normal, I cleaned up the mess that evening, retired early to bed, crying myself to sleep. He returned in the early hours and awoke me by kissing my neck. His affections no longer met any of my emotional needs. I felt almost numb. I responded in the way that had now become the normal – robotic, feeling-less response to his affections. I turned my head to one side as he carried on kissing my neck and shoulders. I stared at the window and thought how dark it still was in the early hours as it came into late autumn.

One of the hooks from the curtain pole had become unthreaded and I made a mental note that I would take the curtains down to wash them and fix the problem. I lay flat on my back dressed only in a washed out grey bra and large pair of peach coloured knickers. The only physical response I made was to remove my knickers from one leg as he worked his way down my body kissing me as if he thought it was giving me pleasure.

After cumbersomely taking one leg out of my knickers, I lay down flat again as we had sex. Sweat dripped from his brow as he grunted, thrusting on top of me as I lay like a bag of wet flour. He roughly grabbed my breast from my bra as he climaxed, then climbed off me and went to the bathroom, saying not one single word. The long distant memory of passion between us in the hotel, was so far away and so hard to believe it was once my actual life, and not a dream. I now lay like a piece of meat to be used on order then kept for further convenient use. I lay there for a while, making the effort to only close my legs as he returned from the bathroom. He climbed into bed and prodded me saying "Wash."

Without response, I got up and showered, as I now fully understood the now 'normal' process that had become our sex life. I sat on the floor of the shower in no rush to return to be in bed with him. Even though it was only five in the morning, I decided to dress and enjoy some time on my own. I found myself reminiscing about the days when I lived alone and enjoyed my own company and rules. I turned on the music and danced around the house as tunes played through my earphones. I pottered around the house cleaning and moved the occasional table that housed the photograph, to one side in a small attempt of defiance. It did not belong in the centre of the room.

My relationship had now moved to another pace - I no longer wondered if I had made the right decision to be with him but was sure it was the wrong one. My life felt like a spider's web in which I had trapped myself inside as prey.   Standing at the bedroom door, I watched him sleeping for a few seconds. I watched his breathing and could not see any movement from his chest and for a split second the thought that he might be dead passed through my mind, and I felt elated. Adrenalin rushed through my body, but within a second, he had moved his arm and was clearly very much alive and the elation turned to anxiety.

He awoke that morning and kissed me on the lips saying, "Good morning, baby," as he went out into the yard to smoke a cigarette. We had different perceptions of what our relationship had become. I made him coffee as he went into the room, sitting on the sofa with the lap top on his knee, as he transferred money from my account to his mother's.

"Thank you. I love you too much," he said smiling as he took hold of the coffee cup. Thoughts passed my mind of spilling the hot coffee to stop the transaction from going through, but that was a fruitless plan. I watched him as he mumbled to himself while on the computer. I noticed that the hairs on the back of his neck and his sideburns were overgrown. Stubble on his face was ragged and uneven. His smartness that I had once admired had now gone. I could no longer see any of the qualities in him that I had once seen.

He caught me staring at him and simply laughed in a forced manner and turned back to the computer. I attempted to make conversation by talking about how I had gone to see Belinda. I told him how she had no money and was renting out her room and how Temarh had gone to study in Edinburgh.

"She is a foolish woman and she deserves all that she gets. I do not know how he tolerates her - she should be grateful that he has stayed with her," he answered, as if my conversation had angered him. The atmosphere became intense and neither of us spoke for a few moments.

"Why are you drinking water with lemons in instead of tea?" he asked without looking up from the screen.

"I read somewhere that it is a form of detox? It cleans your skin, so thought I might give it a try," I answered.

He continued to stare at his screen as he started to laugh. "Well, if you have read it then it must be true. How do you detox with a cup of water when you drink like an old sailor? Perhaps the lemons are magic lemons? Perhaps they will cure you of your old dirty skin?" He put down the computer and stood to his feet still sniggering to himself.
"Echo! Remind me to buy ten thousand lemons so I can have a pretty wife?" he shouted to the wireless device as he left the room.

I avoided being around him for the rest of that day. I called in to see Mum who was busy with friends and did not appreciate me calling unannounced. I decided I would walk Rue, allowing me a purpose to stay away from the house. I took him to the beach and threw his ball as he playfully fetched. The sea air was so refreshing, for a few moments I felt as if I were in another more peaceful world. I had missed Rue's company so very much, I had missed walking him and spending time with him. Dogs love you unconditionally. They do not judge or care about what you have or how you look - they just love you as you are. I watched as Rue ran around wondering if that was why Rue did not like Hammett? Could he sense the bad in him that I had been to blind to see? I called back at my Mum's to return Rue and he leapt with joy to run and greet my father who eagerly awaited his return. I hung up the leash and explained that he may need a drink as he had been picking up his ball in the sand. I left their house with a heavy heart at the thought of going back to my home. My father stood on the step waving as I closed the gate.

"Things won't get better if you don't make them better. Life is too short to be unhappy - just look at your mother she has made being miserable into an art!" he said.

"I know, Dad. Don't go on - I will sort things," I answered with very little belief in my own words.

My head begun to hurt as I set off home. I wondered if I had some kind of brain tumour as I felt like I had suffered from a permanent headache for weeks. I rummaged through my purse for more painkiller's while trying to accurately recall the time I had taken the last dose.

Darker nights had begun to settle in and as I walked home the streetlights came on. Children ran around in groups dressed in fancy dress for Halloween. I watched as they called from house to house calling, "Trick or Treat," as people answered the door to hand them candy. As I approached our house, I could see Hammett talking to a woman with two small children as they stood at the doorstep. The children were dressed as witches with pointed hats, capes and broomsticks. The woman was dressed all in black with a hairband with cat ears on top. She had black cat whiskers drawn onto her face. As I got closer my heart raced as she turned and I recognized her face.

"Janice! I didn't realize you lived around here?" I asked.

"Trick or Treat? Hello Monica, what a small word we live in? I hadn't realized this was your other half until we got chatting. What a lovely little home you have. You are such a 'big miss' at work, but I hear you are onto bigger and better things? So nice to hear."
I looked at Hammett as he handed the children candy whilst avoiding eye contact with me.

Janice was positively high with excitement as she told me she had been promoted to Junior Vice President due to her achievements on getting the Briggs and Lace contract.

"I owe a lot to you Monica, because I know you did some of the ground work for that which set me in good stead," Janice verbally rubbed my nose in the dirt as she said it.

"Well it has been a blast and we must catch up again sometime. Bring your lovely husband - we can make it a foursome - it will be such fun. Come on girls, we have houses to visit and spells to cast" she said as she ushered the children down the path wiggling her tail that hung from her suit, giggling as she walked away shouting, "Ciao, ciao!"

By the time the gate had closed, Hammett had already gone into the house and into the kitchen to light up a cigarette. The atmosphere in the house was palpable as I followed him into the kitchen. I stood in the doorway, unsure of how to start the conversation to explain my lies. Hammett stared at me for a minute, not blinking or speaking. He blew the smoke from his cigarette across into my face.

I stuttered my words as I tried to explain why I had lied about my work. My words were quickly halted as Hammett took a cup from the drainer and threw it across the room, hitting me in the face then smashing to the floor. I felt as if my eye socket had cracked as pain seared through my head. He ran across the room grabbing my head and pushed my face into the frame of the door. He went to hit me again but I moved quickly as his fist hit the wall. He screamed out in pain as he let go of my hair to grab his wounded hand. I ran from the kitchen towards the front door. Within a split second, he was behind me as he kicked me in the back and I fell to the floor.

The Halloween bowl with the candy was strewn over the floor and a photograph of Rue that was once on the passage wall was now on the floor with the glass smashed. As I lay in the mess I could hear children coming up the path giggling and shouting, "Trick or Treat?"

Hammett held my head to the floor, picking up candies and forcing them into my mouth.
His teeth were gritted as he chanted, "Trick or Treat for the witch." I choked as he forced sweets with wrappers into my mouth.

I turned my head and pushed him away from me as he stood to his feet. I tried to get to my feet, too, as he stepped back, but was stopped as he put his foot onto the small of my back, forcing me back to the floor. He stood for a few seconds staring at me then took a deep breath and spat in my face.

"You are a liar and a whore and you brought me here to trap me. I was happy before I met you. You have ruined my life," he said as he turned to walk away. I continued to lay still. To my regret, he came back and with full force, he kicked me in the stomach, then calmly turned and left the house.

Chapter 10

"Hello? Is there anyone there?" There was a large bang that sounded as if it was inside my head.

"Hello? Is there anyone in?" I heard a voice shout, followed by another loud bang. Silhouettes of people stood at my front door blocked the sun from blinding my half-opened eyes. I realized I had been lying on the passage floor all night. As I stood to my feet, I felt an unbearable sharp pain in my back and shouted out.

"Are you okay? Is everything alright?" I heard the voices shouting through the letterbox. As I stood to my feet I could see more clearly the silhouettes were those of two policemen stood at my door. I felt dazed as I tried to undo the lock on the door. I heard the voice of an old lady ask, "Is Monica alright, there?"

It was the old lady from next-door, trying to find out what the police presence was for.
I heard a policeman say, "She is fine, everything is fine please go about your business."

I was walked to the living room and handed a drink of water by a police officer who attempted to find out the cause for my injuries. She took some gauze from a bag and taped it over my eye apologizing if she caused me pain. I winced as she dressed it.

I could hear voices talking in code over the radio that she had on her belt. I could hear the word ambulance and back up. After a few moments my head seemed to clear, and by then my house was full of people, including my father and three more policemen. The policewoman who was sat by my side asked me if I had any idea what had happened to my husband? I explained that I had not seen him since we had argued.

"Do you feel okay to come with me? There has been an accident and I am afraid your husband has suffered severe injuries.

"Hammett? Hammett! It's me, it's Monica. Can you hear me Hammett? Can you see me? Can you talk? Try and keep calm and tell me what's happening. These people are here to help you - to help us both."

It was the early hours of the morning on first of November, the rain fell that day like an icy winter's day. Blood mixed with the rainwater on the paving below his feet. He stood facing the railings. He held onto them like a caged animal as he shouted "Daye, Daye, Daye." He stared forward at the bars. I was only able to see the left side of his face. He raised his left leg and then lowered it, then again. He kept repeating this simple process as if it was a complex challenge. He screamed out as he lifted his leg the pain clearly unbearable, "Daye."
"Do you have any idea what he is saying, Monica?" The policewoman asked me as I walked slowly and cautiously towards him.

"He is shouting for his mother," I answered, feeling sick at the desperation that my answer reflected. The policewoman put her hand on my shoulder to remind me that she was there.

"Don't get too close, Monica. Keep the distance you have now. We need you to remain safe."

Two more police cars pulled up behind the police van, their sirens silenced following a hand gesture of the already present crew. The situation was volatile; no-one knew what had happened and no-one could get close enough to him to find out. His level of aggression was immense, his disturbed state evident.

"Please, Hammett, talk to me? These people are here to help you. Hammett, you are injured and we need to help you." An ambulance turned the corner and reversed into the car park, twenty yards from where he stood.

The ambulance crew are here. We must let them do their job," the police officer held my arm to guide me away.

"Ambulance on standby," a message came onto the police radio.

"It's time to move to a safe distance, Monica.

"Please, Hammett, please?" I cried out. In that instance he very slowly turned his head towards me.

I could hear myself scream but no noise left my mouth. It felt like time had stopped as I wretched and vomited. The socket of his left eye was smashed so badly it was difficult to see where his eye once was. A large pocket of skin had formed a bag of blood that hung from his face like something from a horror film. Blood poured from his mouth as he shouted, "Daye, Daye, Daye." With what seemed like hours, but merely only seconds, three police officer grappled him to the floor. He screamed in pain as he was searched and walked a few short steps to the awaiting stretcher. The policemen held him upright at each side under his arms. They had to talk him through the process of taking one step and following it by another. My eyes where so full of tears I could hardly see.

"How the hell is he still alive?" I overheard a policewoman saying to her colleague.

I vomited in the drain, my body in shock and my mind a blur. He was strapped to the waiting stretcher as a large pad was placed gently on his face, while the ambulance men tried to work out how they could attach it without causing more damage. I sat in the back of a police car following a very slow-moving ambulance with sirens blazing, as if it was undecided if to hurry or not. Twice on route the ambulance stopped while the ambulance driver had to assist the paramedic, before they set off again slowly. The police radio blasted into the silence. We were heading to a far-away hospital where there was a specialist head injury unit, but mid-journey it was decided he would not be able to survive the distance, s we were re-routed to the nearest local hospital, where a team of specialists were to be waiting.

For three hours I waited in the Oasis suite of the hospital. Every passing footstep built up the hope of news, but each person walked by. Logic told me he must be dead or I would most definitely have heard something. But surely, if he was dead I would have also been told by now?

My head burst with questions of what could have happened. I had lost ten hours of my life laying in my hallway not knowing what was going on. My life felt like a thousand-piece jigsaw that had been thrown to floor, I hurt all over my body, my head felt as if it was full of water that moved internally on its own. I had no money or possessions to buy a drink or painkillers. Nursing staff had asked if I wanted a drink when I arrived, but very aware of their workload, I politely refused but now realized that was a stupid decision.

I pulled a large cushion from one of the armchairs in the room and lay down in a vain attempt to rest my aching head. The room seemed to sway as I looked around the blandly painted room. There was a picture of a waterfall hung on the wall with a light behind it, giving the impression the water was moving. There were two arm chairs and a large sofa. A cupboard with two doors stood at the rear of the room with old magazines piled up on top.

My mind started to wonder, thinking of how many people had sat where I was, pondering their lives. I felt parched - desperate for a drink, so I wandered out in search of refreshments. I looked around the corner of the door and I noticed two nurses stood at a desk opposite. Fully apologetic that I had interrupted their handover, I politely asked where the nearest vending machine was. I was told that the nearest one was in the canteen, but that the cupboard in the room had a kettle and an array of refreshments that were for my use. Feeling stupid for not looking before, I turned to go back into the suite. As I closed the doors, I overheard the nurses talking in a loud whisper, supposedly to avoid me hearing what they were saying.

"That's the wife. The police are involved as the causes of injuries are still unknown. She has a black eye, I think they're a volatile couple, by the sounds of things, he's in a really bad way. They are trying to stabilize him for transfer, but it's looking more like palliative care at the moment. I think she's in shock, she hasn't even cried or anything - she just sits quietly." The older of the two then went on to hand the other some keys and wish her a 'quiet shift' as she left her duty.

A few seconds later, the second nurse popped her head round the door to check that I had found the refreshments. She informed me that as soon as they had news, I would be informed. I half smiled and nodded as I took the kettle from the cupboard to make myself a tea.

The truth was, I did not know how I to feel, apart from the same overwhelming feeling of emptiness that had I felt for so long. I felt completely lost and alone. My telephone had run out of battery and despite my lonely feeling I was unusually pleased for the peace. I made myself a tea and sat on the sofa, feeling unable to process thoughts of any kind.

I must have fallen asleep, as an hour later my father shook my arm and woke me. He was stood with the nurse that had called in earlier. My father sat beside me and held my hand as the nurse explained that Hammett remained in a critical condition and was too unstable to be transferred to the specialist head injuries unit. She advised that I contact any family members I needed to, as his time alive may be very short.

"I will leave you alone with your family for a while. I know it's a lot to take in. Take all the time you need and when you are ready I will take you to see him," she said as she left. I cuddled into my father crying, and as he always did, he just held me and said nothing.

We were walked along a corridor that led to the Intensive Care Ward. We passed a room in which a mother cried into her telephone explaining that her son had not responded to tests. She could hardly make her words clear through her tears as she spoke.

There were only four beds in the unit and her son was clearly the young boy that lay directly opposite as we entered. Surrounded by charts, tubes and machines, very little of him was visible apart from his jet-black hair, sticking up above a breathing machine.

Photographs depicting his young life surrounded the board above his head. Cards and hearts with the words, 'We love you, Adam' covered every inch of the board's frame.

There was sudden commotion behind us a middle-aged man came through the swinging doors wearing a black motorbike jacket. His eyes were swollen and red from crying. Adam's mother launched at him, beating his chest and pulling at his coat. The nurse attempted to hold her back but he just covered his face and took her punches.

She screamed at him, "This is your fault! Just look at him! Fucking bikes! Why are you not laying there now, instead of him?" She paused for a while as he held her arms; tears ran in free flow down his cheeks. She fell to her knees saying, "Please, God, not my boy."

We were quickly ushered toward Hammett's bed while the nurses attempted to console her. My father had tears in his eyes as the nurse pulled the curtain around the bed to give us some privacy. I stood nervously away from the bed, not daring to touch him or say anything, the nurse came in from behind the curtain and introduced herself as Leanne. She documented readings from machines and changed rates on other machines, then smiled as she left.

Barely any of Hammett's face was visible between masks, tubes and dressings. A tracheostomy tube had been inserted and stood prominently from his throat, attached to a breathing machine. The deafening silence in the room was broken only by the sound of the whirring machines.

My father left me alone with him, and I sat by his bedside all night until the evening of the next day. His condition neither improved nor deteriorated. The consultant gave progress reports every six hours and said that no deterioration was nothing short of a miracle, given the extent of his injuries.

I was well looked after by the nurses, who brought constant refreshments and support. I watched them in their work and was in awe of the brilliant job they did. They selflessly went about their work, supporting patients and their families in the worst circumstances, without fault.

Sitting by his bed with no change, in some way gave me a sense that he was going to be alright, as surely to survive this far and then die, would be pointless. I was soon to be dragged from my sense of reason when activity in the ward suddenly increased and the curtain was drawn around young Adam. The doctors and nurses rushed around in vain to save his life. Adam's mother was taken, screaming into the waiting room by her husband. The two parents looked hollow and grey as we passed them, when we were asked to step outside for a few moments.

When we were allowed to return an hour later, Adam's mother lay on the sofa in the family room with her head on her husband's shoulder. They looked like they had died inside. Her eyes now fully out of tears and her heart in such a faraway place no mortal soul could reach it. They overcome by a feeling of emptiness and desperation which made me feel fearful of life's cruel power.

The space where Adam's bed had stood was now empty and clear of all personal belongings. As if by clockwork, the cleaner arrived and mopped around the bed area, in preparation for the next unfortunate soul.

I walked toward Hammett, who looked unchanged with the rhythmical pattern of the breathing machine now almost becoming a tune, playing over and over in my head. A nurse tapped me on the shoulder, shifting me from my deep thought, she handed me a clipboard and pen with a health questionnaire and asked me to complete as much as I could. I read the first few questions asking basic things like if he had been immunized as a child? The first five questions were simple enough, but I was unable to answer any of them. This was basic information that I should have known as I shared my life with this man. The questions then became more complex until the very last question, which was something that had not even remotely crossed my mind. The question read 'Are you a British citizen?'

I could feel the colour drain from my face, as the concept of financial implications of whether he lived or died where going to be all-consuming. I got a sudden violent headache and a feeling of nausea.

"Are you okay?" the nurse asked, looking at me with my head in my hands.

"Yes, I am fine, thank you. I just have a headache. I think it is because it's so warm in here. I'll go out and get some air."

"Why not go home and have a shower and a rest? We'll ring you if there are any changes. You know, this could go on for a long time. You need to keep your strength up."

I handed her the uncompleted forms, promising to get the information required. I took her advice and headed home.

As I left the ward, the police officer that had been first to call at my home walked towards me.
"Monica, I'm pleased I caught you. Could we go somewhere private so we could have a quick chat?" she asked, smiling.

I could feel the pain in my head thump harder at the very thought of more drama. She took me into a side room, just off the corridor, and sat opposite me across a small occasional table. She leaned in to talk to me, as if to ensure I heard what she had to say.

"As you know, there's been some provisional investigations into the cause of Hammett's injuries. We found an area along the cliffs near Shore Edge around a mile along the cliffs. It's a remote, rocky area, that's known as Lover Cliffs to the locals around here, I believe."

I rudely interrupted her. "Pervert's Cliff," I said, nonchalantly. She seemed startled at my response. "You're obviously not from around here, because the place you're talking about is known as Pervert's Cliff. It's well known for prostitutes and perverts," I said, as though educating her.

She seemed lost for words as she sat back in her chair to compose herself. "Well, regardless of activity that may or may not go on there, we found an area of blood-covered stone, and have a witness who states she saw him walking there in the early hours. At this stage, it's looking as if your husband had an accident and has fallen."

"He is not my husband and who is the witness?" I asked.

"I'm not at liberty to give any details but can confirm she was able to place him at the area at the suspected time of injury. From the forensic evidence, it seems he has fallen and injured himself, and in a dazed state has attempted to get home, making his injuries worse, I fear."

I thanked her for the information and stood to leave.

"Just before you go, Monica, I'm really sorry for your situation, and rest assured that if further information comes to light, we will investigate." She handed me a clear carrier bag full of his belongings, for which I thanked her and left.

I sat in the car, feeling as if my head would explode. I examined my black eye and bruising to my face in the rear-view mirror. I looked old, battered and worn. I opened the seal on the bag and took out his belongings. I looked through his wallet. That was something I had never done before. There was over three hundred pounds in cash which made me laugh out loud as I looked at the petrol gauge in the car that read empty, as per normal. There were a number of receipts, and a small photo of a group of children sat with an older man who sported a large black moustache and beard. The photograph was old and worn. I examined it closely but could not recognize any of the young children or possibly Hammett as a boy. In the back of the wallet was a business card for a bakery in his hometown with a hand-written name on the top, 'Luella.'

His mobile telephone was scratched and the screen broken, but visible. I tried to turn it on but it was out of charge. With the pain in my head becoming increasingly worse, I decided to halt my prying and go home to shower.

After the shower I lay on my bed. The pillow felt like a cloud. I appreciated the comfort of laying down sleeping, compared to the hard chairs in the hospital which I had sat on for the last few days. I took painkillers, plugged in Hammett's mobile telephone and fell asleep.

I slept deeply for hours. I was awoken by the gentle buzzing noise of Hammett's telephone that was now fully charged on the bedside table. The screen flashed with message after message. I leaned over to answer a call as it rang, but it rang off as I picked it up. The name came up as 'Eser' and a number of missed calls and messages also flagged up from him. He had sent a number of requests asking him to call, each message sounding more desperate than the last. I pressed 're-dial' and waited, expecting an international dialling tone. The dialling tone was British and a voice quickly answered.

"Merhaba! Where the hell have you been? I have been ringing and ringing - we need the money. What are you playing at?"

I was lost for words at the unexpected reply. I apologetically pointed out who I was and why I was calling. The man on the other end fell silent for a while, and I had to repeatedly ask if he was still on the line. He eventually spoke, explaining that he would contact Hammett's family and get back to me once arrangements had been made. He asked if I was alright and if there was anything that I needed, he explained that Hammett's mother did not have passport, so would not be able to travel, but he would contact the family and request they visit. He explained that he was Hammett's second cousin and had been close to him since childhood. He said he would be able to answer any medical questions for him and to ring if I needed him.

It was nice to hear a voice of someone who sounded in control. As I lay in bed, I flicked through the telephone not knowing what I expected to find. There was nothing out of the ordinary to be seen. Some texts where in Turkish and I could not begin to understand them, others were boring day to day texts that we all send but mean nothing. His photographs were of us both on holiday - some of me on the beach that I had not noticed he had even taken at the time. My mind started to drift back to that time when I had felt so sure about life and myself. I pondered on how things could go so wrong so quickly, and what had changed to ruin things?

I dressed and decided to carry on with my vigil at the hospital. Despite what had conspired during the past few weeks, I was determined I would stand by him - whatever that may bring. I had made a commitment to this man and backing out was not an option.

Over the next week, I kept in constant touch with Eser with updates of his condition. He agreed to bring photographs of their family to show Hammett, as the nurses said it was so important to keep his mind stimulated, despite his sedated state. The doctors would call around and do a daily set of tests to check the extent of his brain damage. Physiotherapists called twice daily to do leg exercises to prevent muscle wastage. A feeding regime through his nose replaced the fluids to keep up his strength. Despite all of this input there was no change in his condition. I sat by his side and watched for every little flicker of his eyes. I would sit and stare at his face, looking for glimpses of the man that I had fallen for. I thought of Belinda and how, despite having nothing, having a small part in Temarh's life was enough and she was contented.

I so wanted to feel that I was a caring person, but I couldn't shake off the numbness, the pity or the guilt.

The doctors told me, that despite the lack of deterioration, to not build up my hopes, as his condition remained life-threatening. I was given leaflets for different support groups. On the back of one of the leaflets was an advertisement for funerals, with the caption stating 'a full funeral could start with as little as six thousand pounds'. I could not afford to even keep my home now, so the thought of six thousand pounds was crippling. It was as if any financial worry should not count at such a time, as life matters more than money. The truth was though, it did count and facing it made me feel physically sick.

I stayed at the hospital by day and went home late in the evening. This particular day I had to leave early, as Eser had messaged to say they would be arriving at six that evening. I had invited them to stay at my house, explaining that it may be a little cramped, but they were welcome. I had cleaned the house and prepared piles of bedding the evening before and shopped for food to ensure they felt welcome.

When I arrived home at six that evening, they were already waiting in the garden of the house. They greeted me with hugs and said how sorry they were about Hammett. Eser was exactly as I had imagined him to look. He was late twenties with dark hair and a precisely trimmed beard. He had travelled from Manchester, where he had lived for three years. He had greeted Hammett's aunt and elder cousin at the airport. Eser had to translate for us as neither of them spoke any English. His aunt was a stern looking woman, with black and grey hair. She had piercing blue eyes and long eyelashes that framed her eyes. She wore deep-red lipstick that was applied perfectly. After many attempts at pronouncing her name badly, we agreed that I would call her 'Mamma M' to make things easier. She inspected my house for dust as she ran her fingers along the window ledges and nodded with approval as my standards met hers.

Eser's younger cousin was in his late teens and was called Recu. He was a pleasant boy with fair hair - much unlike the rest of his family. He was thin build and his arms hung from his t-shirt like a wizard's sleeves. He shook my hand when he greeted me, as if he was unsure of the etiquette of greeting an older woman and did not want to offend.

They unpacked their bags and we headed to the hospital. The environment amazed them all as they went into intensive care, just as I had been when I first walked in. Adam's father stood at the nurse's station, He had brought gifts of thanks for the staff. The nurses asked about his wife and he explained that she was not doing so well, but that it was early days. My heart felt heavy for them. Adam's bed space had now been used by three other people since he died. It brought home to me how fragile life was and how quickly we are replaced.

Mamma M wailed as she saw Hammett and struggled as she attempted to cup his face in her hands. All the machines surrounded him prevented her from being tactile. His eyes seemed to flicker at her presence, but the nurses felt this may be due to the noise she made. Racu stood back as Eser talked to Hammett comfortably, as if he was awake. He seemed very relaxed around him - much more than I had been in the initial stages. We were allowed to stay for only twenty minutes, as the strict rule of only two visitors per bed was applied.

While we visited, the porters and nursing staff were bringing a new patient into the unit. It was a young man who had apparently been beaten in a senseless fight over a girl. The young man had been in surgery, but was expected to make a full, but slow, recovery. His mother spoke to the nursing staff about the mindless bullying attack her son had endured. I realized, that in all of this commotion, no-one had noticed my bruises or black eye. I wondered if my beating was senseless or justified because of my behaviour. Regardless, Hammett lay in front of me fighting for his life. So, my 'if's and but's' were pointless in comparison.

It was late in the evening when we arrived home, and I had picked up a take away as I was sure no-one would feel like cooking. We arrived home and Mamma M took a shower as Eser and Recu chatted in the living room. I asked Recu where his name originated as it was not a typical Turkish name. He explained that his mother was Turkish but his father was American and how he hoped to travel to America one day to meet him. His father's name was Rudi Cannes and they had met when he was on a study tour from university. He chatted about his dream of visiting London and seeing the famous sites.

Mamma M walked into the room as we chatted, quickly halting Recu's conversation. She ranted angrily in Turkish and pulled at Recu's hair as she spoke, as if to chastise him. Eser answered her in Turkish trying to calm her outburst and Recu got up and left the room. They carried on arguing and Mamma M waved her hands around in a dramatic manner, she stormed over to the television where the picture of the stones on the beach saying 'marry me' stood proudly.

She picked it up waving it in the air saying, "ridiculous," and laughing.

Eser became very stern with her and raised his voice, she said nothing further and left the room.

I asked him what was wrong, and he explained that Recu's birth was as a result of a holiday fling that had brought much shame on the family at the time. He said that Mamma M was very old fashioned in her ways and did not agree with Recu talking about his father.

"Why did she talk about the photograph?" I asked.

Eser stuttered and paused before he answered. "She was just referring to Recu's mother never marrying, that's all."

We returned to the hospital the next morning and agreed to take turns visiting in two's. I sat in the family room as Mamma M and Eser went in to visit first. The consultant had just finished the ward round and called in to ask to speak to me. He shook hands with Recu and I introduced him as Hammett's family.

"Oh, I'm pleased we have blood relatives here. It makes consent much easier. We have examined Hammett this morning as you know, and I have to say this man is nothing short of a miracle to survive these injuries. He is, however, still very ill, but has remarkably become more stable. We have a surgeon coming to the hospital tomorrow who is willing to work with our surgeons to see if we can repair some of the smaller vessels that continue to bleed in his brain. I have to say, this is not ideal, but as Hammett's condition proves to be fragile, allowing him to be moved is the only option we have. If he remains as he is now, we plan to operate tomorrow morning. One of my juniors will be in shortly when all of the paperwork will be prepared for you to sign."

Recu quickly went into the unit and told Mamma M what had been said. In her usual dramatic manner, she scuttled to the family room and began to wail and rant. Eser tried in vain to calm her down quickly following her into the family room. She ranted away for a few moments, then turned to me and said, "His wife and children should be here - not you!"

I turned around to see Eser hold his head in his hands and Recu stand like a rabbit caught in the headlights. A thousand questions ran through my mind, but the words would not leave my mouth. I stuttered but could not speak. Eser shuffled Mamma M out of the room, as she carried on waving her hands in the air and ranting undeterred that my world had just been shattered. Recu followed her as he was ordered to by Eser. Eser tried to hold me, repeatedly saying how sorry he was, I pushed him away and sat down unable to comprehend what I had just heard.

I sat for a moment and nothing was said between us. The silence was overpowering.

"Tell me - I need to know?" I asked Eser.

He stood up and kneeled down in front of me. "It is not what you think. Monica. Hammett loves you and only you. He knew if he told you of his past you would not want to be with him."

"Does he have children?" I asked.

Eser was silent for a while until he admitted that Hammett had two sons, aged one and eight. He said that Hammett had been told to marry by the family and that it was not out of love.

"Oh, well, that's alright then. Just leave a pregnant woman with a child to manage alone just because he was unhappy! Are you seriously trying to make excuses for him?"

"Meeting you changed his life, Monica, he was in love for the first time. He wanted a new life, a life with you. He was the happiest I have ever seen him when he met you."

Chapter 11

I left the hospital and did not look back. Unsure of where to go, I drove for miles, my eyes filled with tears. My life felt like the greatest mess and the saying, 'there is no fool like an old fool' rang through my mind. The warnings people had given me were now resounding, 'how could anyone be so blind?' I had literally lost everything - self-respect, friends, my job, money, the cost was too much to bear.

I drove to Phil's house; it was the only place I knew to where I felt I could escape. My car was more abandoned than parked as I ran to his front door and banged hard on it. I was so relieved to see Phil's silhouette through the door as he came to open it. "Hold on, where is the fire? You'll have the glass out if you knock any harder."

Phil took one look at me standing there, "Oh, hello local bag lady," he said laughing.

I walked passed him into the house saying, "Don't be funny, Phil, I'm not in the mood."

"Well, hello, to you, too! I thought you had fallen off the planet, seeing as though I have not heard a single word from you since that delightful meal? Despite me sending you an invitation to my one and only wedding," he said as he held out his hand to show off his engagement ring.

"I know, I'm so sorry. I am literally the worst friend. In fact, I am the worst at everything."

Phil rolled his eyes, "I see we took our self-pity tablets this morning, then?"

I started to cry and blurted out the full story as Phil sat and listened quietly only with the odd roll of his eyes. He passed me tissues as I told him how my life was beyond repair.

"Is he going to die, do you think?" he asked.

"I don't know to be honest. He just looks helpless and fragile in there, with all of those machines. When I look at him laid there, he is a stranger to me," I answered.

"Well, he is a stranger, pet. He is not the man you thought you had met. He has been living a lie." Phil brutally brought perspective.

"Yes, but so have I! It is such a mess - two wrongs don't make a right - they make a mess," I said as I slumped back into the chair.

Phil's telephone rang. It was Warren asking how his day was going and telling him he would be home a little late. I watched Phil smile as he answered the call - he was pleased to talk to him. He was happy as they made arrangements for an evening meal and made small talk just to hear each other's voices.

"Buy enough for three, pet - we have a guest - Monica is here," I overheard him say as he left the room.

"Yes, she's fine. Things have just been a bit shit and I think she needs an escape. I will hun yes and that would be lovely. See you then. I love you too. Bye for now."

Phil came back into the room and sat next to me. "Well, sweetheart, we need a plan and you need a soak in the bath – Warren's orders." Within minutes the bath was run and the aroma of bath oils floated through the air. Phil had laid out a fluffy blue dressing gown and some white slippers that he had stolen from a hotel, still in the wrapper.

"You go and relax and I'll get us a drink," he said.

I felt a wave of tension lift as I sunk into the sweet-smelling hot bath. For a few seconds my life went on hold, as I thought of nothing but how relaxed I felt.

Phil came in the bathroom, carrying two large glasses of wine and sat on the floor next to the bath.
The make-up I had used to cover the bruises to my face had washed off.

"He is handy with his fists then, is our Hammett?" Phil asked.

I was just about to make an excuse for him when Phil butted in. "Don't bother with the, 'it was because of this and because of that' excuses you were about to give me there. I have been there pet, remember Pablo? He hit me once and I found myself apologizing for antagonizing him. I can't believe it when I look back now; we are so blind in love. I was convinced he was a nightclub owner. I was such a fool. I only found out he was in prison and not Barbados doing a deal because he sent me a letter with a prison stamp on it. He was only from Manchester, even his accent turned out to be fake. I even got him a car on credit, can you believe?"

As always Phil made me laugh. I had not laughed in so long. I winced with the pain in my ribs as he went on to tell me how he tried to tell the car company he had been conned by someone from the mafia in an attempt to get out of the debt.

"He has hit you pretty hard, there'" Phil said as I climbed out of the bath. He turned the mirror to show me the bruises to my back.

"It's not right, pet. Nothing gives anyone the right to do that to anyone."

"I know," I answered ashamedly.

I went into the living room where Phil had lit the log burner and scented candles; the room looked so cozy.

"I've got you a pair of Warren's pajamas, they'll drown you, but they'll do for tonight because you are staying here - I insist. Tomorrow we'll decide what to do and I will help you."

I started to cry again.

"Stop blubbering - we have a plan to make," he said as he cuddled me.
"He hated you because are gay," I said as I lay on his chest.

"I know he did hunny but he wasn't the first and sadly he won't be the last, so we don't care what he thinks, do we?"

Warren came in that evening carrying a box containing two large cream cakes for us. He came straight over to the sofa where I sat and kissed the top of my head and handed me the box.

"Hello, Monica. It's so lovely to see you and I am so pleased you came here. You know, Phil is the love of my life, and I know how much he loves you, which makes us practically family. So, you just sit there and relax while I make you a hot milky coffee and rustle us up some dinner. How does pasta sound?"

Without waiting for an answer, he headed off to the kitchen carrying the shopping.

"He does the most amazing tomato sauce," Phil said as he ate his cream cake. We chatted for a while, until Warren returned with two large milky coffees in clear glass cups with chocolate shavings sprinkled on the top.

"Ooooh… what a treat!" Phil said as he handed him his.

"Well, we all deserve a treat sometimes," Warren said as he handed me my drink.
"We have all been in the room with no door at some time in our lives, Monica. We are just blessed to know that real loved ones wouldn't leave us in there. Things will sort themselves out in time, but for tonight you just recuperate a little - it will help you see things more clearly."

That evening we sat and ate our meal, chatting and laughing as I sat at the dinner table wearing Warren's oversized pyjamas. They had my bed made up with clean sheets and painkillers appropriately obviously placed next to my bed with a glass of iced water with lemon.

"Don't worry about disturbing us if you need anything - just give us a shout, God bless," Phil said as he closed the door.

That night I slept better than I had in months and awoke to find my clothes washed and ironed and in a neat folded pile at the end of my bed. Warren had gone to work and Phil had made fresh orange, toast and coffee. We chatted about my plans for the future.

"I'm not sure what to do, but I know I need to get myself in a better place – mentally, before I make any big decisions about life."

"Well, that's easier said than done. But you know, if you ever need anything, you just come here?"

I left there that morning feeling more positive and ready to face things.

I returned home to find Mamma M in the house alone. She did not welcome me or speak, but by her general demeanour I got the impression she was angry with me.

"Where did you stay last night?" she eventually asked bluntly.

"With friends, not that it's any business of yours" I answered.

She glared at me, "You are a liar and a prostitute and you do not deserve a good man such as Hammett."

I felt anger well up inside me. "How dare you?" I answered. She simply turned her back on me and left the room. I followed her in anger as she walked into the kitchen and looked through the cupboards trying not to acknowledge my presence.

I slammed the cupboard door shut in front of her.
"This is my house and this is my kitchen. Don't you
dare think you can come in here and talk to me like
that? If you think Hammett is a good man, then you
are a foolish woman. He is a liar and a bully; you do
not know him as well as you think you do."

She turned to face me defiantly; bile welled up in her.

"I am no fool, but you are a stupid, middle-aged
woman who leaps at the first sign of so called, 'true
love,'" she said and laughed out loud.
She continued her vile rant as she invaded my
personal space, forcing me to retreat like a wounded
soldier.

She carried on with her verbal onslaught. "You are
old and washed up! No man will want you, so you
come to Turkey wearing your stupid bandana and
waltzing around the restaurant like you owned the
place. You think because you have a bruise on your
face it makes you a victim? Well, grow up! This is real
life and to have man like Hammett you must be a
better wife. Look at this house - it is dirty and you
have no money. You lied to him to trap him, now he
is hurt and you wash your hands of him. You make
me sick and I will not stay another minute under your
roof."

She left the house taking only her small handbag and slammed the door as she left, the house shaking like an aftershock. Part of me sympathized with her; we had different perceptions of who we were in life. She would defend him regardless of his actions, and for that I felt a weight lifted from me, as I then knew he was not completely my responsibility.

Within minutes, I heard my telephone ringing from my bedroom. I ran to catch it before it rang off. As is usually the case, it stopped ringing just as I reached it. It had come from a withheld number, which usually meant it was the hospital. I attempted to call back the intensive care unit, but it was constantly engaged. I changed my clothes and grabbed my purse and keys and attempted to ring again as I left the house. Eventually, a nurse answered and informed me that Hammett was returning from surgery. She apologized that she had not been able to contact me, but had contacted Eser to inform him also, and that he was *en route* to the hospital.

It was a race against time to see who would arrive at the hospital first. Feeling like the gods were against me, I hit every red light and traffic delay on the way. I abandoned my car in the nearest space and ran in without getting a ticket. I breathlessly ran along the corridors trying desperately not to knock into people as I hurried. A nurse wearing scrubs passed me and reminded me that running was not allowed and could cause an accident. I apologised and continued to run as she shook her head with disgust at my ignorance.

As I reached the unit, I could see Eser waiting in the family room with his hands clasped together.

"Oh, my God! Has he died?" I asked frantically holding my chest.

Eser stood to his feet, "No, no, I am waiting for news. Mamma M is with him - they are trying to wake him to see how he responds. The doctor has been in earlier to tell us that the surgery went remarkably well."

I breathed a sigh of relief, "I should be in there with him."

"There's only one person allowed in. Mamma M had to put on a special gown and mask. They want her to give him simple instructions in Turkish to see if he has understanding. It's better she's in there."

With no cruel intent from him, I felt as if I had just been placed in my appropriate position in the pecking order and had no grounds to question my appointed position.

We seemed to wait for hours without any news. Eser was fully aware of my argument with Mamma M and made it clear he would not take sides. He said he knew that she could be difficult at times, but as family she must be his priority. He had made arrangements for them to stay in Manchester but said this may take a few days. He asked politely if I could tolerate her for a few more days until things could be sorted. Trying to take back some control, I agreed that it would be fine, although inside I felt like crying.

By late evening that day, Hammett was awake and able to communicate by eye movement. The doctors discussed a regime of reducing sedation once the swelling from the operation had been reduced, and if all stayed well, to take out the tracheostomy tube.

Mamma M took total control from that point on and all care decisions were put through to her. She would stand vigil from early morning until six in the evening, when I would then take over to stay for a few hours. I was happy to go home late most days, as my house no longer felt like my own.

The week she was to stay turned into a month. She rearranged the furniture in my living room and changed the placement of the utensils in the kitchen. She did laundry for them all but would bag my clothes in a bin liner as if they were rubbish. The household bills soared as the heating and hot water were permanently on full. Every day I would reset the thermostat and every day she would change it back. I found myself sleeping with the windows wide open unable to sleep as the heat soared through my house. The food bill was enormous, and I found myself at the store everyday replacing food that they had eaten. Eser often promised to discuss finances but the conversation never happened.

I looked forward to evenings with Hammett. I found them cathartic as I was able to talk to him about our issues and he was unable to verbally respond. Sat by his bedside one day, I talked about his wife and children and how hurt I had felt, asking why he had lied? I knew he was unable to answer and in some way, I was pleased, as deep down I understood he would have no excuse that made it all right. Of the little information I had about them, I worked out that he must have left her pregnant and with a small child to manage on her own.

"How could you even do that to them? Did you ever love them? Did you ever truly love me, come to that?" I asked.

To my shock, I felt his hand squeeze mine. I shouted for the nurse to tell her what he had done. She explained that it was his way of responding and was completely not phased. The evenings with him became the best part of my day, when I would read him the newspaper and talk about better times. The hand squeezing became a regular thing and within days he was able to smile.

Within two weeks they had taken out his tracheostomy tube (with Mamma M holding his hand) and he was very much breathing on his own. He could not talk for a number of days, but gradually he built up his strength. He was transferred into a rehabilitation ward where visiting rules were more restricted. Without any real discussion, we came to a natural agreement that Mamma M would visit in the specified day visiting hours and I would visit on the evening. The staff in the unit would comment on how amazing Mamma M was with her intense approach on rehabilitation. She discussed how she worked relentlessly for three hours daily encouraging him to do exercises and feed himself. They named her, 'the inspirational Mamma.'

Weeks went by as gradually he built up his strength. He was able to walk, although initially with a walking frame. His ability to answer simple questions with a 'yes' or a 'no' took weeks with intensive speech therapy. Within two months, he was talking again. His speech was fully understandable, although slurred. He had intensive psychological support to help him understand the effects of his injuries. We had a meeting with the psychologist; it was the only time I sat calmly in a room the same time as Mamma M. He explained to us that although Hammett presented himself as 'normal' there would be lasting effects from his injuries, such as behavioural changes. He gave an example of someone who was once mild mannered may become the complete opposite and ill tempered. I laughed at his example to which Mamma responded with a scowl.

"He will always require care to monitor his behaviour for the rest of his life," the physiologist said, butting in on our non-verbal dispute.

"What kind of care?" we both asked at the same time.

"General support with daily life. I am aware that he looks at ease within this setting, but he has no pressures of daily life here. He may struggle with things we find simple - such as shopping and employment."

We both said nothing; he was not returning the same man he was before the injuries. Mamma M ran from the room wailing and crying. I had no tears and her dramatic outburst meant nothing to me. The psychiatrist asked if I needed to go after her and see if she was all right to which I just shook my head.

"Can I ask quickly if you would speak to the immigration and finance advisor?"

He handed me a business card with the contact details.

"Yes, of course," I stuttered. "Can I just ask - what it is in regards to? I mean I know it is around visas and things, but just to clarify?"

"It's really not my department to advise, but it is in regards to payment for healthcare. Please do not worry - the advisor is a lady and she is very good. She will be able to advise you on all you need to know." I thanked him and left the ward without saying goodbye to Hammett. Mamma M had already arranged a lift and gone.

I could not face going home that evening, so I called at Phil's house. Warren informed me that Phil had gone off cake tasting for the wedding and was not at home.
"Didn't you want to go with him?" I asked.

"God, no! This is his fourth tasting session. He's milking it for all that it's worth. I went to the first one thinking it was a one-off deal and that was enough for me. Phil has decided the cake is now going to be a surprise for me. I'm to have no part in its creation, which is fine with me. Cake is cake to me. I will let him enjoy that part, if it makes him happy. Come in, I'll make us a coffee while we wait."

I followed Warren into the kitchen where he made a creative-looking latte in a coffee machine. Much to my delight, he placed a raspberry macaroon on the side of the saucer to accompany the coffee. I smiled when I saw it.

"They're Phil's favourites. I buy them from a small Italian bakery near to where I work."

"What is it you do Warren?" I asked.

"I deal with finances for large companies when they are merging. It's not exciting, but it's well paid and I get to manage my own time which is nice. I get to travel to interesting places, which I ashamedly admit I once found a chore, but since meeting Phil it has become the highlight of my work. Phil loves to travel and he is a fun travel companion." He smiled when spoke of Phil.

"You two are such a lovely couple. I can honestly say I have never seen Phil so settled and content in life as he is with you."

Warren took two more macaroons from the box and put them on my plate.

"Please eat them or I know I will, and I don't need the weight. Monica, we have all had our share of rubbish relationships. I used to believe that you have to kiss a lot of frogs to find your prince, but the truth is - a frog is a frog. After years of failed relationships and bad decisions in life, I've realized people only treat you as you allow them to. Gay, straight, English, foreign, men or women it doesn't matter. It's how we think about ourselves that counts more than anything. Sadly, you met Hammett at a time when you felt low and saw him as the answer to everything when the reality is you are your own answer, so things were destined to be difficult. We all do it - we start a relationship and on a daily basis we make excuses and we fix the cracks in the hope that things won't fall apart. Like all things meant not to be held together, eventually something gives and we are forced to face reality. We avoid looking at the bigger picture, because it's easier not to face what we might see. Don't get me wrong - because I'm not here to judge. Hammett may not be a bad man - I have no idea - but you are not good for each other. A partner should tell you to take care when you leave the house, not control where you are going. Being with someone you truly love is about empowering them, not overpowering them. Anyway, enough of my lecturing, another coffee?" he asked.

Phil arrived home and excitedly placed ten small boxes containing cakes onto the table. "I've had the best day. I still can't decide between red velvet and chocolate with raspberry."

"Why don't you have a layer of each?" Warren asked.

Phil stared at him as if he had just invented chocolate.

"Now, that's why I love you," he said as he kissed Warren. "You're still going to have to wait until the day though, it's going to be the best surprise."

Phil walked over and kissed my head saying, "Hello, sweet, how are you, how are things? Has Warren been looking after you in my absence? Did he give you a macaroon?"

I laughed. "He did, yes, and he's been lovely."

"How is our little angry liar? Still recovering, I hope?" Phil asked rolling his eyes.

I told them about what the psychologist had said and about the immigration advisor.

"Oooh… that doesn't sound good, does it Warren?" Phil said alarmingly.

Warren was quick to chip in, "Don't scare the poor girl to death Phil. It may be nothing, Monica, just for filing, but let me go make a quick phone call to a man I know who specializes in this kind of thing to see if I can get some clarity for you," with that Warren left the room.

"You are so lucky to have met Warren, Phil. He is a lovely man."

"I know hinny I can hardly believe my luck. He loves me for being myself, can you believe? I can actually see a future with him. I want to grow old with this man. He does so many things to make life good - I have never felt like this about anyone in my life."

Warren came back into the room after calling his friend. Phil sat with his hand over his mouth in a show of unnecessary drama as Warren told me to prepare for a hefty bill. He explained that it was likely they would bill Hammett for all of his health care expenses that could run into tens of thousands. Hammett had no insurance and no long-term visa. Financially, things were already out of control but this news was a game changer.

When I got home that evening, Mamma M had moved out of the house. She had taken all of her belongings and some of Hammett's too. She had thankfully taken the picture of his deceased friend and my home looked almost back to normal. I felt a sense of relief at the normality as I took down the plastic roses from the wall that I had almost forgotten were there.

I showered and that evening decided to take stock of my life, starting with my financial situation. I took a pad and paper and wrote down all that I owed and put it into order of things that must be paid soon and things that I had time to prepare for, or brush aside for the time being. The outlook did not look promising, but the fact that I had faced it gave me a sense of achievement and most of all, some control.

The following evening, I attended the hospital early to meet with the advisor before visiting Hammett. Eser agreed to accompany me and was already waiting when I arrived. The advisor I had arranged to meet was unavailable and so we waited a while until a replacement could be found. A young man turned up around forty minutes after the agreed time. He was very apologetic and said that he was unaware of the case, but as he had shadowed in the role as the immigration health advisor for the Trust, he would be best placed to step in and fill his colleague's absence.

He looked through Hammett's health file quickly, looking especially closely through three sheets of figures on the final three pages. He stroked his non-existent beard as he said, "Yes, well, that all looks in order."

"What looks in order? I'm not sure why I have been asked to come here?" I pointed out.

He sat back in his seat and began to discuss that as Hammett was not a British citizen, then his health care was not free under the National Health Service. He had not registered at a general practitioner and due to his illness, he had outstayed his allowed time in the country. He asked if we had been married or intended to marry, and if Hammett owned any property in the country?

"I'm afraid to tell you, that Hammett has a substantial health bill," he said leaning forward as if to emphasize his seriousness.

"How much is substantial?" I asked while bracing myself for the answer.

"Well, you must take into consideration the high level of care needed at the initial stages of his surgery, and now of course, his rehabilitation, which is an ongoing cost."

"How much is substantial?" Eser asked again.

"It's just over thirty-seven thousand pounds, with an expected cost of above forty thousand pounds with the predicted need for rehabilitation." Every single word he said after that was a blur. Health care had always been something I had taken for granted, never needed or wanted to think about it. My ignorance had caught up with me in the worst way.

I made my excuses from the meeting, saying I needed to get some fresh air, as I felt rather ill. I left Eser to discuss issues further with the advisor.

I returned to the ward to find Hammett sat playing cards with another patient. He seemed pleased to see me, turning his head and smiling. Rather than finishing his game, he threw his cards onto the table and stood to his feet. The lady he was playing against held her hand of cards in the air to emphasize his rudeness at walking away mid game.

"Finish your game, it's fine," I said.

"No, I don't want to. She doesn't matter - she is a stupid woman - she can't talk anyway," he said as he rudely walked away.
For so many months, the darker side of Hammett had been masked due to illness, but there and then I saw a glimpse of the real him reappear. I had taken so long in making any kind of decision for the future, until that very moment when I knew I did not want to waste any more of my life with this man.

Within two days, Mamma M and Eser had ensured that Hammett was pronounced well enough to fly home and plans for this were in place. The bill for his care was thankfully in his name only and something that he was to carry with him whenever he earned enough to pay. Mamma M decided that he could get better and cheaper rehabilitation at home, surrounded by his family and her say was final.

By the Monday of the next week flights were booked and all of Hammett's things were taken from my home. I had decided not to go to the airport, as it would not be comfortable. I decided to go to the hospital to say my goodbyes and visited for my last time on the Sunday evening. Hammett was watching television when I arrived and did not respond or look at me as I sat next to him.

"Hello, how has your day been?" I asked.

He did not answer but continued to stare at the screen. The nurse came over to tell me that his physiotherapy session had been cancelled today due to his aggressive behaviour. She asked if he had ever behaved this way prior to his injuries? I explained that he was prone to outbursts of bad temper and violent behaviour. I tried once again to talk to him but he continued to ignore me and look away. I tried to broach the subject of us splitting up but I could not find the words. I told him that I had applied for a new post in an up-and-coming advertising company and that I had been short-listed for interview.

"You're going there to meet other men," he said without looking at me.

I was taken back by his reply, "What? Why would you say that? I need a job, I have bills to pay. This is what I do?"

He sat silent for a few moments, then picked up the remote control and turned the volume on the television up until it was deafeningly loud. The nurse came over and took the remote from his hands and reduced the volume.

"He sat still for a moment then turned to me saying, "You go to the bank for money, you will not go to a new job."

I could not think of a sensible answer for him, it was as if I were talking to a moody teenager.

"Well, I'll have to work and I am trying to explain that I will not be coming to Turkey with you when you go home," I said calmly.

He seemed to have no understanding that I was talking about leaving him. He turned his head towards me and smiled. He started chatting and asking how my day had been. It was as if he had not even heard my conversation at all or pretended not to. He started to talk of what we would do when I went over to stay with him and I simply nodded in agreement, knowing nothing I said made any difference.

On the table next to him was a pile of magazines. The title on the front page of one was, 'Taken for a fool by my Egyptian lover' I turned over the magazine to avoid looking at it. Women that I once would have judged as foolish for their actions, were normal women just like me. These women were simply looking for someone in life in order to feel complete just as I had. I felt so foolish and empty that even the thought of starting over in life was daunting.

I left the ward that evening contemplating my life. Walking away from him on the ward had not felt like I had said goodbye. He had not understood our conversation and clearly thought I would be joining him in Turkey.

I sat that evening feeling very emotional and self-pitying. I did anything I could think of to pass the time, including walking Rue and applying for more jobs. Dressed in casual wear I heard a knock at the door and someone came in walking and shouting, "I hope you're decent," as he entered.

"Phil! What are you doing here?" I asked in amazement.

"Well, the thing is, my best friend needs closure and I don't think she is up to the job on her own. I'm here to take her to the airport to say her goodbyes and close this chapter in her life for good. God bless us and save us because then, at least, she can move on," he said as he held his hands together in prayer.

Tears welled in my eyes, "Are you sure this is not the worst idea you have ever had?" I asked.

"It's not my idea, sweetie. I would let you slam the door in that man's face. It is Warren's idea, and as much as I hate to say it, he is often correct. So, we're tight for time, so pop on a sweatshirt to complete that ensemble you are wearing as stylish as it is and we best get our skates on."

When I got into the passenger side of the car there was a packet of tissues and a small paper bag in the door panel, containing three macaroons.

"Is this Warrens idea, too?" I asked.

"No, sweetie, that was mine," Phil said smiling, obviously pleased with himself.

We arrived at the airport with only minutes to spare. We ran through the corridors of the terminal. "This way sweet," Phil said as he jumped onto the moving stairs. I followed him and became out of breath while I tried to keep up with him.

Hammett was sitting in the cafeteria with Eser and Recu. I walked towards him as Phil hung back twenty yards behind me. Eser stood to his feet and hugged me. "We will give you some privacy," he said as he ushered Recu to his feet. Recu shook my hand as if we were business partners, then uncomfortably kissed me on the cheek.
Hamett did not seem to care too much that I was there and carried on drinking his drink.

"I just came to say good bye and see you off," I said.

"I would offer you a drink, but Eser said it is nearly time to board the flight," he answered.
"That's okay, I didn't want a drink," I answered.
There was a short pause of silence between us.
"I really do wish you well and that things are good for you at home. Maybe you could open another restaurant? You should spend time with your family, children grow up so quickly, you have so any memories to make with them," Hammett did not answer.
"You have been given a second chance at life. It is a gift - I truly hope you spend it well," I said as I stood to my feet.

I saw Mamma M appear across the cafeteria. She charged towards us but was stopped in her tracks by Eser.

"It's time for me to go, now. Be good in life and take care," I said as I kissed him on the head and walked away without looking back. I knew I would never see him again and that he didn't understand this.

Tears flowed from my eyes and as I looked at Phil, he was crying too. We both started to laugh in something of a state of hysteria.

"Why the hell are you crying?" I asked.

"Well, I wanted to look in the shops, but you were quicker than I thought," he said laughing. "No, seriously, I'm proud of you, sweet. Now let's go home and pick out a cake."

Chapter 12

The music started to play and we stood to our feet. Warren and Phil stood holding hands as they made their vows. Phil's mum could be heard wailing as his uncle Raymond tried to console her. Warren laughed during his vows as Raymond could be heard saying, "Pull yourself together, Joyce. You're letting our side down."
The full room exploded in laughter as his Aunt Pauline responded saying, "Frigging hell, she'd have to do something serious to make a show of our lot!"

"If we could have silence?" the registrar requested, reminding everyone to be civil during the fits of laughter.

We danced into the early evening and Phil's three-tier red velvet cake was the highlight of the table. As the evening came to a close, we stood outside the floodlit castle to wave off the happy couple. My phone buzzed on silent.

"It's your phone, Mum. You should answer it – it might be about that contract?" Lilly said as she stood at my side.

"The contract will still be there in the morning, some things are more important," I said as I took the confetti from my purse ready to throw.

"Would you like some confetti to throw, Belinda?" Grace asked her mother.

"No, thank you. I don't do confetti," she answered, with her lips pursed, refusing to show any signs of happiness for the newly-weds.

Handfuls of pink and red confetti were thrown into the air above the beaming couple as they got into their rainbow car adorned with ribbon. The light rain created puddles festooned with the tiny paper pieces turning the pools red like rose petals.

We watched them disappear into the distance then got into our cars to get out of the rain.

"Where are we going, Mum?" Lilly brushed the water droplets from her jacket.

"Let's get Rue. I could do with a walk."

"But it's raining, Mum?"

"I don't care all's right with the world, I'm going to enjoy every minute. I feel alive."

As I drove, I thought of Phil and Warren and with joy I wished them all the best for them both. I was starting a new chapter in my life, too. Things would be good.

The cost wasn't the thousands of pounds of debt I found myself in; it wasn't the shame, the heartache or the pain. The cost was my life, it was for the love of a man who was a monster and the memories of this that would remain in my mind for a long time. It was time I would not get back, the knowing that at some point in this toxic relationship we loved each other and the feeling of loss.

23774157R00168

Printed in Great Britain
by Amazon